POISON AGENDAS

A low, throaty growl sounded from the trees to their left. The shadowrunners whipped around toward the sound just as a whirlwind of gray fur exploded from the shadows. It slammed into Natokah, and the shaman and his attacker went tumbling down the slope. Natokah yelled in pain and surprise, and the other shadowrunners sprang into action.

Orion drew his sword and leapt down the slope in a single motion. He tumbled in midair to land lightly on his feet close to where the creature had Natokah pinned to the ground. It was massive, as long as the shaman was tall, and it definitely outweighed him. The beast was all powerful muscle, with a blunt muzzle filled with sharp teeth, and heavy slashing talons on all four paws. Orion attacked and left a bloody gash along its flank, drawing its attention away from Natokah. The beast turned with a fierce growl, jaws flecked with white foam and red blood.

POISON AGENDAS

A Shadowrun™ Novel

STEPHEN KENSON

A ROC BOOK

ROC

Published by New American Library, a division of
Penguin Group (USA) Inc., 375 Hudson Street,
New York, New York 10014, USA
Penguin Group (Canada), 90 Eglinton Avenue East, Suite 700, Toronto,
Ontario M4P 2Y3, Canada (a division of Pearson Penguin Canada Inc.)
Penguin Books Ltd., 80 Strand, London WC2R 0RL, England
Penguin Ireland, 25 St. Stephen's Green, Dublin 2,
Ireland (a division of Penguin Books Ltd.)
Penguin Group (Australia), 250 Camberwell Road, Camberwell, Victoria 3124,
Australia (a division of Pearson Australia Group Pty. Ltd.)
Penguin Books India Pvt. Ltd., 11 Community Centre, Panchsheel Park,
New Delhi - 110 017, India
Penguin Group (NZ), cnr Airborne and Rosedale Roads, Albany,
Auckland 1310, New Zealand (a division of Pearson New Zealand Ltd.)
Penguin Books (South Africa) (Pty.) Ltd., 24 Sturdee Avenue,
Rosebank, Johannesburg 2196, South Africa

Penguin Books Ltd., Registered Offices:
80 Strand, London WC2R 0RL, England

First published by Roc, an imprint of New American Library,
a division of Penguin Group (USA) Inc.

First Printing, January 2006
10 9 8 7 6 5 4 3 2 1

Copyright © 2006 WizKids, Inc. All rights reserved

ROC   REGISTERED TRADEMARK—MARCA REGISTRADA

Printed in the United States of America

PUBLISHER'S NOTE
This is a work of fiction. Names, characters, places, and incidents either are
the product of the author's imagination or are used fictitiously, and any
resemblance to actual persons, living or dead, business establishments,
events, or locales is entirely coincidental.
    The publisher does not have any control over and does not assume any
responsibility for author or third-party Web sites or their content.

To my friends; my parents, George and Lynn; and to Christopher, most of all.

ACKNOWLEDGMENTS

When you write in the Sixth World of Shadowrun®, you stand on the shoulders of giants. My deepest thanks to Mike Mulvihill for his trust and guidance, to Sharon Turner Mulvihill for her input and expert editing, and to Bob Charrette, Tom Dowd, Paul Hume, and Jordan Weisman for starting it all and each helping in their own way to bring the Sixth World to glorious and gritty life. Without them, this book wouldn't exist, and I would have missed out on a whole lot of fun along the way.

TRANS-POLAR
ALEUT

ATHABASKAN
COUNCIL

QUÉBEC

SALISH-
SHIDHE
COUNCIL

ALGONKIAN-MANITOU
COUNCIL

Seattle

TIR
TAIRNGIRE

SIOUX
NATION

UNITED CANADIAN
AND AMERICAN
STATES (U.C.A.S.)

UTE
NATION

Denver

CALIFORNIA
FREE STATE

PUEBLO
CORPORATE
COUNCIL

CONFEDERATED
AMERICAN STATES

AZTLAN

CARIBBEAN LEAGUE

**NORTH AMERICA
AS OF 2060**

Copyright 2005, WizKids, Inc.

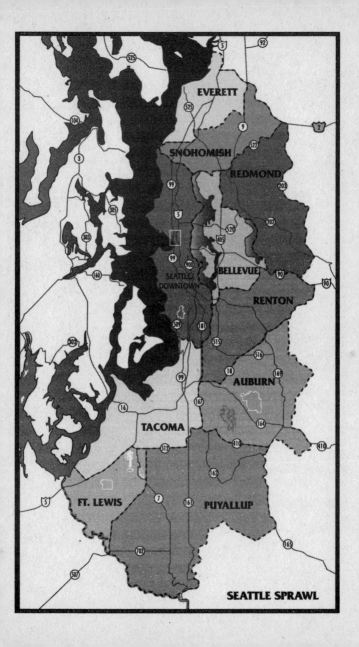

SEATTLE SPRAWL

1

Juan Espinosa wasn't a particularly brave man, which was now something of a problem. As he made his way along the upper level of the mall in the Aztechnology Pyramid, Espinosa loosened his tie, trying to relax its grip on his throat. And despite the mall's perfectly controlled environment, he found he needed to wipe away sweat beading on his brow.

The evening weather outside the broad windows was clear—a welcome change from the previous four days of rain in the Seattle Metroplex. The nice weather seemed to have enticed everyone outside—to enjoy some shopping inside. The mall surged with shoppers. Men and women wearing the latest in corporate fashion, like Espinosa, teenagers wearing the latest in synthdenim, synthleathers, neospandex or urban tribal wear. A scattering of metahumans stuck out in the crowd, but most of the shoppers were human. Many metahumans couldn't afford to shop at the Aztechnology Mall, which was just as the mall's owners preferred it.

Espinosa fought the urge to look behind him for about the fifth time, glancing instead into the window of Lordstrung's and trying to see in the reflection any sign that he was being followed. He couldn't tell if anyone seemed interested in him, but that didn't mean they weren't there. He spotted a row of vidbooths across from the food court and unconsciously quickened his steps. He slid into an empty booth and pulled the transparex partition closed, fumbling in his pocket for his credstick. He slid the short plastic rod into the reader beside the flatscreen display, then tapped the telecom number he'd been given into the keypad. He prayed he remembered it correctly, since he hadn't dared to entrust it to his headware memory.

The moment it took for the call to be connected seemed to last an eternity, and Espinosa risked a glance out the transparent partition. Still no sign of any surveillance, but there were plenty of people milling about, any one of whom could be the one.

"Feeling a tad nervous, Mr. Espinosa?" a voice said, and the startled Aztechnology exec spun back toward the screen. It displayed a kid-trid cartoon image of a pretty girl with a heart-shaped face, impossibly large eyes and a tiny mouth curled up into a smile. The face was framed by flowing black hair, swept back and held in place by a headband shot through with silvery circuit patterns.

"There's nothing to worry about," the sweet voice continued, carrying through the speakers in the booth. "Everything is under control and going according to plan."

"Of—of course," Espinosa stuttered, swallowing convulsively and wiping his sweaty palms on his thighs.

"We're ready to go. Just leave the booth and head over to the Soya-King stand. We'll take care of the rest."

"But what . . ." he began, but the flatscreen had already gone black. The connection had been broken, and Espinosa knew the number wouldn't work a second time. All he could do now was what he had been told to do. So he pulled his credstick from the slot, stepped out of the booth and headed for the Soya-King stand, weaving his way around the scattered mall patrons enjoying a late dinner.

As he approached the stand, a tall elf wearing a leather jacket bumped against him. Espinosa spun, a hasty apology on his lips.

"Hey, watch where the frag you're going!" the elf snarled.

"I'm sorry . . . I—"

"Yeah? You're gonna be more sorry!" The elf reached out and grabbed the collar of Espinosa's suit jacket. He yanked the hapless man toward him so that they were almost face to face, though the elf stood a good ten centimeters taller. A sizzling pop jerked his gaze down to the elf's hands, and he saw the stun gun a split second before it hit him.

The elf jammed the small weapon into his gut and Espinosa convulsed as the electric charge slammed into him. His limbs flailed spasmodically, and he heard several people shout as they noticed what was going on. Then the elf dropped him to the floor, and he wasn't aware of much more. All he could think was, *What went wrong?*

From where she stood near the food cart, Kellan Colt watched the exchange between Espinosa and his elven assailant. The elf dropped the stunned corporate suit, backed away a step, and then took off through the crowd as several people rushed to see what was happening. Kellan was at Espinosa's side in an instant, crouching beside him. He groaned, but was clearly out of it.

"Oh my God!" she said, loudly enough for the people nearby to hear. "Somebody get help! Somebody hit a Panicbutton!" Several people in the crowd reached for their phones to punch the Panicbutton service key incorporated into every cell device, and alert the authorities to the problem. With a deft movement, Kellan reached into Espinosa's jacket and "took out" the small, pagerlike device she'd kept palmed.

"DocWagon is on the way," she said, holding out

the signal device so other people could see it. "Everybody step back and give this guy some breathing room until they get here." The crowd, grateful for someone to tell them what to do but still curious about what was going on, began to reluctantly pull away from Kellan and Espinosa, continuing their muttered conversations. Then their attention was drawn by a sound coming from the main corridor of the mall.

Kellan glanced up as a force of Aztechnology security double-timed it around the corner into the food court, shouting for people to get out of their way. The crowd instantly parted as the guards swung their rifles in an arc ahead of them, laser sights painting red dots on the walls and floor. Their body armor was matte-black ballistic cloth, their helmets showing blank faceplates of opaque transparex, no doubt with heads-up displays providing tactical feeds.

"Everybody back!" the lead guard barked, emphasizing the command with a wave of his gun. The crowd immediately complied, leaving Kellan crouching beside Espinosa's sprawled figure. She immediately got to her feet and took a few steps back, keeping her hands where the guards could see them. It was possible they were packing rubber or plastic bullets in those state-of-the-art assault rifles, but Kellan doubted it. This was trouble.

The guards immediately surrounded Espinosa, the lead man leveling his weapon at Kellan. She didn't need to look down to know there was a targeting point painted on the front of her white tank top as the man took a cautious step forward.

"All right, miss," he began, "put your hands behind—"

Suddenly there was a loud bang at the far side of the food court and the security guards all spun in the direction of the noise, weapons at the ready. One of them fired off a burst, and people screamed and fell to the floor. The bullets went high, leaving ragged holes in the far wall and taking out part of a neolux sign in a shower of sparks and fluorescent gel. They were definitely not firing rubber bullets.

Except for flicking a quick glance toward the gunfire, Kellan kept her gaze on the security guards. When the Aztechnology men turned, she raised one hand and spoke a phrase in a fluid language. The exact sound of it was lost in the noise, but her words wouldn't have been intelligible even if the mall had been completely silent. The lead security guard spun back toward Kellan just in time to see her hurl a fist-sized ball of light at his feet. He didn't even have time to call out a warning.

The ball of light burst in a soundless explosion, engulfing the security guards and Espinosa in its radiance. Kellan focused on confining the burst to the few meters occupied by the armed men. A few mall patrons were caught in the blast of the spell as well, but it couldn't be helped; she had made the area of effect as small as she could. Where the golden light struck, people crumpled, like puppets with their strings cut. The Aztechnology guards and half a dozen mall patrons simply dropped to the floor, the only sounds being bodies hitting the tile and guns clattering down beside them.

Kellan pulled a compact earpiece and throat mic from the pocket of her jacket and slipped it over her right ear as an elf and an ork came charging toward her. The shocked crowd mostly stayed where they were, crouching or lying on the floor, or hiding behind small tables and chairs.

"Jackie, we're fragged," Kellan said into the mic. "Security made us. We're headed for the pad. Tell Max to hurry."

"Understood," replied a woman's voice. "I'll give you what cover I can."

"What happened?" asked the elf who had incapacitated Espinosa. The other man, a burly ork, crouched beside the unconscious company man.

"I don't know," Kellan said. "They must have been tipped off. They were in position and armed for bear—not like regular Aztechnology security."

"He's out cold," the ork announced, after checking Espinosa's pulse to make sure he was still alive.

"He'll stay out for a while, too," Kellan replied. "Pick him up, we've gotta get the frag out of here."

Without further comment, the ork lifted the unconscious suit and tossed him over one broad shoulder with little more effort than picking up a child. Kellan touched a hand to her throat mic.

"Jackie, we've got our boy, but we need the quickest way out of here."

"There's an emergency exit to your left," the decker's voice replied after a second. "About four meters down the corridor. It's eighteen flights up to the pad."

Kellan nodded. "Let's go," she said to the others, and headed down the hall at a quick trot.

"Stop!" a voice shouted as they reached the emergency door. Kellan turned and saw another team of armed security guards headed their way. The lead guards raised their weapons.

"Go!" she shouted, and the elf hit the emergency door running. An alarm began sounding through the mall as the door flew open with a bang. The ork followed, carrying the unconscious Espinosa, with Kellan right behind. She dived through the doorway as shots ricocheted with loud *cracks* off the metal frame and the ferrocrete wall. She pushed on the door to shut it, then abandoned her effort and let the hydraulics close it behind her as the three of them took the stairs at a run.

"Jackie, we—"

"I'm overriding the maglocks on all the emergency doors," the decker interrupted, "and shutting down the elevators, but that's only going to slow them down, not stop 'em." Behind them, Kellan could hear the guards hitting the door with something heavy.

"Roger that," Kellan replied.

"Fraggin' heavy suit," the ork puffed as they hit

the fourth flight of stairs. "He could definitely cut down on the nachos."

"I could say the same for you, G-Dogg," the elf said with a wicked grin, taking the stairs two and three at a time with long-legged strides.

"Then maybe you should carry his fraggin' butt, Orion," G-Dogg shot back.

The door one flight below them burst open and a couple of shots *whanged* off the metal railing and smacked against the ferrocrete stairs.

"Stop where you are!" a guard yelled.

"Keep going," Kellan told her companions. The elf hesitated for a moment, glancing back at Kellan, then G-Dogg barreled past him and he turned to follow. Kellan raised her hand and spoke the same phrase she'd used in the food court. Another glowing ball of mystic energy leapt from her fingers as three guards charged into the stairwell. It burst in a soundless explosion that laid the guards out unconscious.

Kellan started running up the stairs again but stumbled, catching herself on the railing and breathing heavily. The two stun spells in relatively rapid succession had taken their toll. She wasn't sure she'd be able to pull off another one, and hoped she wouldn't need to. She focused on keeping her legs moving and catching up with the others as they pounded up the stairs.

The emergency door at the helipad level yielded to G-Dogg's shoulder, and the three of them burst out onto the narrow landing pad, the lowermost on the outside of the Aztechnology Pyramid. Built in the style of the step pyramids of the ancient Aztecs, but on a much larger scale, the building featured several helipads on the broad flat "steps" between levels, suitable for landing small commuter tilt-rotor and vertical take-off or landing vehicles. As they emerged onto the pad, a Federated-Boeing tilt-rotor angled in for a landing. The white vehicle looked like a stubby plane or an elongated van, with short wings that rotated to angle the powerful turbofans so it could make vertical descents. On the side was emblazoned the red cross-and-caduceus logo of the DocWagon corporation.

"Security is closing on your position," Jackie warned.

"Roger," she replied. "Let's get the frag out of here."

"Aw, just when things were starting to get interesting," G-Dogg joked, hefting Espinosa into a modified fireman's carry.

The side door of the tilt-rotor slid open as it touched down on the pad, revealing a massive troll who barely fit in the frame of the door. His shaggy head and curling horns brushed against the roof as he crouched there, the backwash from the engines whipping his long hair. He wore an overcoat heavy with armor plating, and painted with mystical designs and symbols. One hand clutched an ornately carved staff topped with a crystal. His free hand waved the team toward the aircraft as it touched down.

They ran out to meet it, G-Dogg in the lead. The troll hopped down from the doorway, moving aside to allow the ork to load his unconscious burden aboard.

"Lothan, trouble is right behind us," Kellan yelled over the roar of the turbofans, and the troll gave her a broad, tight-lipped smile in return, only his lower tusks jutting up over his lip.

"I think we can deal with that," he replied in a bass rumble. He pointed his staff at the wall of the building and shouted four words that Kellan didn't recognize. The crystal at the end of his staff glowed, and then radiated a shimmering beam of blue-white light. Lothan swept the light along the length of the wall, and wherever it touched the exterior surface of the building a thick sheet of ice appeared, covering both the emergency exit and the main doors onto the landing pad. The translucent wall was at least ten centimeters deep. The troll mage grunted in satisfaction as he admired his handiwork.

"Nice," Kellan said. "You're going to have to teach me that one."

Lothan smiled. "All in good time. Now let's be off. I believe we've outstayed our welcome."

Kellan and Lothan climbed on board behind Orion, and G-Dogg slammed the door shut. The engines roared and they lifted smoothly off the pad, turning away from the Aztechnology Pyramid and toward the downtown heart of the Seattle Metroplex.

"Hang on," said a new voice on the commlink in

Kellan's ear, this one low and gruff. "We're out of here." The VTOL surged forward as the wings rotated and the engines put on a burst of speed. Kellan grabbed for a seat and its safety harness, glancing out the window as the air suddenly became unnaturally dark around the aircraft.

"Uh-oh," she said, "Lothan, company!" A powerful howl of wind sent the VTOL slipping sideways, the engines whining to compensate as they lost altitude. Kellan felt her stomach lurch and grabbed for a stable handhold.

"Damned guard elementals," Lothan growled, as he was thrown roughly against the cabin wall. "Max, keep us stable!" he shouted.

"What the frag do you think I'm trying to do?" came the angry reply from the flight deck. "Lothan, get rid of this thing before it drives us into the ground!"

"Watch carefully," Lothan said over his shoulder to Kellan. Then the troll mage planted his feet as firmly as possible on the tilting deck of the aircraft. He held his staff vertically in both hands in front of him, closed his eyes and concentrated, muttering arcane-sounding phrases under his breath as the crystal on the staff once again glowed with power. Lothan focused his will on dismissing the air elemental buffeting the VTOL, as the wind howled like a living thing outside the cabin.

Kellan slid over to the window and looked outside, focusing her perceptions past the mundane. She ignored the glow of the city lights below them, the spotlights focused on the carved crystalline sides of the pyramid. She blocked out the lurching and swaying of the cabin as she gazed into the swirling windstorm outside and saw, with eyes other than the physical, what was there.

The elemental spirit was a thin figure clad in dark rags that were swirling and flapping in the wind along with its long, wild hair. It looked like a hag, with a pointed chin and nose, its eyes black pits lit by glowing spots of electric blue light. It opened its mouth and screamed with the wind, extending hands like bony claws as it fought against the aircraft's engines and against the power of Lothan's banishing spell.

Pressing one hand against the window to steady herself, Kellan gathered her will. With her other hand, she traced a pattern in the air, a faint glow trailing her movements and leaving mystic symbols shimmering before her. She spoke the words of the spell, then jabbed her fingers toward the air spirit. A bolt of light leapt, straight and true as a shot, piercing the spirit like a spear. The elemental shrieked, then dissipated like smoke in the wind, which died away with the last sound of its cries.

The aircraft righted itself and began to climb, heading out over the metroplex. Lothan opened his eyes and settled into an empty space on the bench seat next to Kellan.

"I had the situation under control," the troll said, and Kellan shrugged.

"I just figured we needed to clear out before any more guard spirits showed up, and you were keeping that thing busy."

Lothan nodded. "Sound reasoning. But beware interrupting a banishment. Such a spell might not always be so successful."

Gee, you're welcome, Kellan thought, but contented herself with muttering, "I'll keep that in mind."

Apparently satisfied, Lothan keyed his commlink. "Jackie, what's our status?"

"I'm spoofing the air-traffic control grid so the Azzies won't be able to track you," the decker replied. "By the time they scramble any pursuit, you should be well out of range."

"Excellent." Lothan spoke to the flight deck. "Homeward, Max," he said, "and we can dispose of this business."

"You got it," the pilot replied. "Looks like we've got clear air. We'll be at the meet in no time."

"Then, perhaps," the troll said, "we can find out where exactly our plans went awry."

Lothan had come to the same conclusion as Kellan and probably everyone else: something had gone wrong, which could only mean an information leak, and that meant someone had sold them out. If that was true, then somebody had to pay.

2

Silver Max expertly guided the tilt-rotor along the edge of the metroplex downtown and east toward the Redmond Barrens. Years ago, before the Awakening, the Barrens had been a prosperous area. But the chaos of the past fifty-plus years had taken their toll on some places more than others. Economic and political upheavals had transformed Redmond from an affluent tech-rich community to a depressed and hellish district of the Seattle Metropolitan Complex, under the administration of greater Seattle.

That meant a life of neglect for the inhabitants of the Barrens, mostly nonentities so far as the metroplex government was concerned. People without SINs, System Identification Numbers, didn't exist in the government's databases. That meant the government wasn't obligated to provide them with anything, including basic services and legal rights, and could ignore them as long as they didn't cause trouble for "real" citizens. So Redmond was filled with condemned and abandoned buildings, and condemned and abandoned people who were carefully watched from the outside by the security forces working for the government and corporations. Redmond was left to quietly rot.

That arrangement suited shadowrunners just fine. They took advantage of existing outside the government system to sell their services to the highest bidders. They did the dirty work—the jobs no corporation or government could publicly acknowledge needing done but that were so very necessary in the cutthroat world of modern business. Places like the Redmond Barrens represented hell to many, but served as havens for shadowrunners, places where they could go about their business undisturbed, so long as they were discreet.

Max set the VTOL down in an abandoned lot well inside the borders of Redmond. The dwarf rigger killed the landing lights on his approach, bringing the aircraft in using nothing but instruments. It would have been difficult for an ordinary pilot, but not for Max, since he was plugged directly into the aircraft's systems through his vehicle control rig. The VTOL's sensors were like his own eyes and ears, its wings like his limbs, its engines like his muscles; so Max guided them down safely in the pitch-black night, moving as surely as a man walking through a familiar room by dim moonlight.

As soon as they touched the ground, the team

sprang into motion. Espinosa was still deeply unconscious, so G-Dogg hefted him again while Orion slid
open the hatch and hopped out. He covered the area
with a flat-profile pistol, alert for any signs of trouble,
his superior metahuman vision easily piercing the
gloom. Kellan, G-Dogg and Lothan followed close
behind.

"Jackie," the troll mage announced, "we're on the
ground. Status?"

"No signs of pursuit," the decker's disembodied
voice replied. "At least, nothing you're going to have
to worry about. I've made sure air-traffic control
doesn't have a lock on your location. It's a good bet
the Azzies are putting out feelers, though, so don't
linger."

"We have no intention of doing so," Lothan said.
"Max, clear out and meet us at the rendezvous when
you've taken care of our ride."

"Roger that," the dwarf replied. Kellan could just
see Max through the tinted windows of the aircraft,
lying back in the pilot's seat, cables trailing from the
jack behind his ear. He looked like he was asleep.

Orion slid the hatch closed and the engines began
to whine as the team backed away, then the tilt-rotor
lifted off with a wash of air, dust and loose paper
and plastic from the parking lot. In a few moments,
it cleared the tops of the nearby buildings, then the
wings rotated forward and it headed off into the
dark, its running lights coming on once it was a short
distance away.

A van awaited them in the alley running along the back of the lot. The local gang had been paid to ensure that nothing happened to it. A few moments later, the shadowrunners were on their way through the streets of Redmond with G-Dogg at the wheel, Orion riding shotgun and Kellan and Lothan squeezed in back with their "guest."

"That must have been quite the stun spell you used," the troll commented, observing Espinosa's condition.

"Well, I wanted to make sure I took down the guards." Kellan knew she sounded defensive. "I knew it wouldn't hurt Espinosa. He'll come around eventually."

"It wasn't a criticism, my dear. I think it was rather well done, all things considered."

"Thanks." Kellan was taken aback; Lothan so rarely handed out compliments. She had been learning magic from the old troll mage since shortly after she'd arrived in Seattle, just a few months ago. When she got involved in a fight outside a club where G-Dogg occasionally worked, her survival instinct forced a powerful, unsuspected magical talent to the surface. G-Dogg introduced her to Lothan, who volunteered to take her on as his apprentice in the mystic arts. Magicians were valuable in the twenty-first century, both in and out of the shadows, which gave Kellan an edge in finding work. Before coming to Seattle she had been strictly a small-timer, pulling just enough runs in Kansas City to make ends meet.

With her newfound talent and a couple of month's worth of big-time runs under her belt, she felt she was ready for something more challenging.

"Did you see any sign that Espinosa was being watched?" Lothan asked. Kellan shook her head.

"I don't think so. I mean, he didn't know we were going to fake an attack so we could 'evacuate' him with the DocWagon chopper, and he did seem kind of nervous—but that's no big surprise for an exec looking to jump ship to a rival company."

Lothan nodded. "True. Did you assess his emotional state?"

"No, it all happened too fast, and I stuck with the plan, which meant limiting the magic I did inside the pyramid."

"Well, I think we should avail ourselves of the opportunity to do so now, don't you? Just in case." He waved one hand toward the unconscious suit in invitation for Kellan to proceed.

"Okay," she said. She took a deep breath and let it out slowly, willing herself to relax. Kellan was finding it difficult to learn astral perception, what Lothan and many other magicians simply called the Sight. It took concentration, practice and, most of all, focus, to open oneself up to the images and impressions of the magical world. At first, Kellan only managed it spontaneously. Now, she felt she was getting the hang of it.

As she willed her perceptions to shift, Kellan's vision went slightly out of focus and she became aware of softly glowing haloes of light around each person in the van. Their auras, their life energy, were now visible to her magical senses. Orion's aura was particularly bright in her peripheral vision; he was an adept, gifted with magical physical abilities of his own. Because he was a powerful magician, Lothan's aura should have been blindingly brilliant, but Kellan knew the old mage deliberately concealed much of his magical power beneath a facade she had yet to learn to penetrate. Lothan's staff and amulet, however, shimmered with power.

Kellan turned her attention to Espinosa, examining the unconscious man's aura. It was strong and healthy, indicating he'd suffered no serious harm in their escape from the Aztechnology Pyramid. There were some dark spots here and there, particularly around Espinosa's head. Kellan knew these dark spots were signs of cyberware implants, alterations to the body that put it out of synch with the aura. Espinosa had a datajack behind his right ear, and a few other headware augmentations; fairly common equipment for a man of his position and income.

The emotional surface of the aura was placid—little surprise, since he was deeply unconscious. Were Espinosa awake, Kellan could have read impressions of what he was feeling from studying his aura. It was an inexact science that she was still learning, but she could already pick up more than surface emotions. Lothan was able to read an amazing amount of detail from observing someone's aura, though he combined it with a talent for reading people in general.

Rather than looking at the company man's emotions, Kellan focused on finding telltale signs that Espinosa was under the influence of any sort of spell, or that his soon-to-be-former employers might be using magical means to track him. She saw no lingering spells in his aura, no threads connecting him to distant rituals and no spirits hovering about.

"He looks clean," she said.

"I agree," Lothan replied. "How long until our meeting with the Johnson?" he asked the runners in the front seat.

"About two hours." G-Dogg answered without taking his eyes off the road.

"Good. That should give us some time to make sure our guest is awake and in good condition when we make the exchange, and perhaps ask a few questions before our principal arrives to take possession."

"You think he sold us out?" Orion asked, lifting his chin toward Espinosa.

"I don't know yet," Lothan rumbled. "But I intend to before our business is concluded."

Espinosa regained consciousness soon after the shadowrunners reached their destination, one of Redmond's many abandoned strip malls, its storefronts covered with sheets of construction plastic and layers of gang graffiti. He seemed quite surprised to find himself alive, and to be tied to a chair in the middle of an otherwise empty room.

"What is this?" he asked, tugging at the bonds securing his hands and feet.

"This," Lothan replied, rising to his full height of three meters, his horns nearly brushing the ceiling, "is payback for the trouble you've caused us, Mr. Espinosa."

"What trouble? What are you talking about?" Despite the cool temperature of the dimly lit room, Espinosa began to sweat.

"I mean the fact that Aztechnology security knew about your imminent departure, that they were ready and waiting for us, and that someone must have agreed to cooperate with them. To act as bait."

"I—I don't know what you're talking about," the exec replied, glancing nervously around the room. "My new employers hired you to get me out of Aztechnology, not to attack me. . . ." He struggled weakly against his bonds.

"That was part of the plan," Lothan said. "We chose to make it look as if you needed medical attention so that we could whisk you away in a purloined DocWagon VTOL. We didn't fill you in on that part of the plan because we wanted it to look real, and to avoid any potential security leaks. . . ." The troll's voice trailed off and his eyes narrowed, making him look very dangerous.

"You're looking very warm, Mr. Espinosa," he

purred sympathetically. "And your aura is quite turbulent. Fascinating thing, the aura. You can learn so much from it." He took a step closer to the company man. "For example, you can see when someone is telling the truth or when they are lying. You can even reach into the aura and *twist*. . . ." He extended one massive hand toward Espinosa's sweat-sheened brow.

"They didn't give me any choice!" Espinosa blurted out, squeezing his eyes shut and flinching away from Lothan. "They said if I didn't cooperate, they would . . . Oh, *Madre de Dios*. . . ." He lapsed into muttering fearfully in a mix of Spanish and Nahuatl as Lothan approached.

"Well?" the troll asked.

"He's telling the truth," Kellan said, "and is scared out of his fraggin' mind."

"Very good—though I'd say it's rather obvious." He looked down at the whimpering company man with an expression of disgust. "Contain yourself, Mr. Espinosa. We're not going to hurt you." At that, Espinosa dared to raise his eyes to look at Lothan, his pitiful sounds stilled.

"You—you're not?"

"Of course not. You're still a valuable commodity, after all. You're going to get your wish and find yourself placed with a new employer as soon as they arrive to collect you, which should be quite soon. However. . . ." The troll paused for emphasis, turning away from Espinosa slightly.

"However, I want you to keep in mind that it's a small world out there, Mr. Espinosa, and getting smaller all the time. Memories in the shadows are quite long, indeed. Should you find yourself in need of professional shadowrunning services in the future, you'll find that the price has gone up considerably."

The meet went smoothly. Juan Espinosa was soon in the hands of his new employers, who were pleased with the shadowrunners' performance and promptly paid the agreed-upon fee for delivery of the goods.

Later, in a dark corner booth at a local drinking establishment, Lothan divided the spoils. Kellan was disappointed with her payout. As always, Lothan had deducted a percentage of her share as his fee for teaching her magic. Kellan acknowledged that it was what she had agreed to, but still felt it wasn't entirely fair that she did some of the most dangerous work while Lothan got to sit back and enjoy the profits.

"Maybe I should start working some jobs on the side," Kellan said somewhat glumly, looking at the balance on her credstick.

"Dante's Inferno is looking for bouncers," G-Dogg offered helpfully. The ork occasionally moonlighted as a bouncer for various nightclubs, primarily for the opportunity to see and be seen, and to conduct some business. G-Dogg also claimed the work helped to keep him sharp and gave him the opportunity to roughhouse when he was in the mood.

"Thanks," Kellan said dryly, "but I don't think I'm

cut out for being a bouncer. I meant some shadow work."

"Don't get ahead of yourself, kid," Silver Max advised, taking a swig from his tall glass of beer. "You haven't been in town that long, and you've got a pretty sweet deal going with us."

Lothan gave an expressive shrug. "I certainly have no objections if Kellan wants to strike out on her own," he said. "Her business is her own. Though I agree such a decision would be ill-advised."

"Why?" Kellan asked. "You don't think I can handle it?"

Lothan raised one bushy eyebrow. "Frankly, no," he said bluntly. "You have talent, my dear, and real potential, but don't let a few successes go to your head."

Yeah, Lothan is a fine one to be giving people advice on not getting a swelled head, Kellan thought. *If Lothan's ego were any larger, he would need someone else to help him carry it around. But hey, that's one of the things he has me for.*

"I've done pretty well for myself," Kellan said in her own defense, and Lothan nodded.

"Yes, for a novice, but—"

"But nothing!" she interrupted. She suddenly found she really wasn't in the mood to hear the troll mage expound yet again on how she had a lot to learn. "I handled things just fine on this run, and on every other run I've been on. If I hadn't taken down those Aztechnology guards, then G-Dogg and Orion would have been fragged, Espinosa would still be working for Aztech, and they probably would have blown the VTOL out of the fragging sky!"

Kellan had jumped to her feet during her tirade and was leaning forward into Lothan's face, hands braced on the table in front of her. The troll mage didn't flinch as Kellan vented her frustration.

"I was the one who took care of that mess with the Ancients and the Spikes, too," Kellan continued. That caused a slight glimmer in Lothan's eye. He and Kellan were the only ones who knew for sure that Lothan had been working his own deal during that run—something he had not felt it necessary to tell the others, and something Kellan had kept to herself. She wasn't about to blurt it out now, but she didn't mind letting Lothan sweat a little. If he was concerned, however, he didn't show it.

"Are you *quite* finished?" Lothan asked in a low voice, and Kellan suddenly realized she was causing a scene. She abruptly sat down and slumped in the booth, trying to make herself as invisible as possible to the other patrons of the establishment.

"You were fortunate," the troll continued evenly. "*Very* fortunate. But don't confuse luck with experience and skill, my dear, because they are what wins out every time."

"I'm not your 'dear' anything, Lothan, so stop treating me like a child."

"Gladly, when you decide to stop acting like one. If you want to be treated like an adult, then here are some adult realities for you, Kellan. You are quite right. You are not a child, and I am certainly not your parent. You are my apprentice and I am your teacher, and I would be remiss if I did not try to teach you certain things that will keep you alive in the life you have chosen. Ours is a professional relationship. If you are unhappy with it, or if you want to seek other opportunities, then you are free to do so. I feel it is fair to warn you, however," he raised a finger for emphasis, "you will have to seek those opportunities on your own."

Kellan stood up again. "Maybe I'll do that." She punched the PAYMENT button on the screen at the edge of the table to cover the cost of her drink, pulled her credstick from the slot and turned on her heel to stalk away from the table and the rest of the team.

Lothan wanted her to stop acting like a child? Fine. She would show him just what she was capable of doing. Then the arrogant fragger would give her a little respect.

3

Kellan thrust her sword at her opponent's heart, but his blade came up in a graceful arc, swatting aside the point of hers. She quickly brought it up to block the follow-up slash at her shoulder, and then flailed a stroke at her foe's neck. He again blocked the strike easily, spinning his sword to whirl Kellan's own blade out of the way. Then came a lightning-quick thrust, jabbing the blunt tip of the practice blade right into her stomach, just below the ribs.

"Ow!" Kellan exclaimed, taking a step back and rubbing the sore spot.

Orion saluted her with his practice sword before dropping back into an en garde position.

"Again," he said curtly, and Kellan gathered her wits to return the elf's salute and regain a ready stance, sword arm extended, free hand out behind her for balance.

"Attack!" Orion said, and Kellan lunged forward.

Orion twisted his torso to present less of his body as a target, bringing his sword around in an arc to deflect hers by the narrow margin needed to make her miss him entirely. Kellan swept her own sword around in a wide arc, catching Orion's blade as he came in slow, and pushing it aside.

"Good!" he said, coming around and blocking Kellan's swing at his upper body. Then he made a jab at her leg. Kellan dropped her sword down to block it, but Orion only feinted. His sword blazed up and struck Kellan's shoulder with a loud slap.

"Ow! Fraggit!" Kellan yelled at the sharp sting from the rattan practice blade.

"Focus," Orion said. Kellan gritted her teeth and massaged her shoulder as the elf stepped back into ready position, with no indication their sparring was leaving him even the slightest bit winded.

"Again," he said with a nod.

Kellan took a deep breath. She reached up to brush a few strands of sweat-soaked hair out of her face, then returned Orion's salute.

"Attack!" he proclaimed, and Kellan lunged forward. This time, Orion sidestepped her attack and came in with an upward thrust of his blade. Kellan tried to backpedal to get out of the way, but lost her balance. The elf knocked her sword from her grasp, sending it clattering to the floor as Kellan toppled over backward, landing with a thump on the unforgiving wood.

"What the frag was that for?" Kellan yelled, glaring at Orion as she massaged her shoulder, still stinging from his previous hit.

"For not paying attention," he said. "If you want me to teach you how to use a sword, the least you can do is try."

"I *am* trying!"

He shook his head. "You can do better than that." He offered Kellan his hand to help her up, but she ignored it, struggling to her feet on her own.

"Do you have to hit so hard?" Kellan protested.

"It doesn't hurt nearly as much as a real sword would," Orion said without a trace of sympathy. "If this were a real sword fight, you'd be dead."

"But it's not a real fight. It's supposed to be practice."

"It's also not supposed to be easy."

"Fraggit," Kellan said. "Maybe I just shouldn't bother."

She turned toward the door.

"Hold on!" Orion said. "What's really going on, Kel? Are you still hacked off about that drek with Lothan?"

Kellan remained quiet for a moment, but went to pick up her fallen sword. Taking her silence as an affirmative, Orion continued.

"Don't let him get to you," he said. "You know better than anybody what a blowhard Lothan is. He's fragging older than God's parents and he doesn't think anyone can handle anything as well as he can." Orion and Lothan had had their share of disagreements. The elven adept was quick acting and quick tempered compared to Lothan's cool and calculating approach, which took in every possible variable before arriving at a decision.

"I didn't notice you saying he was wrong," Kellan muttered, looking down at the sword in her hand.

"What, about you not being ready to set up business on your own?"

Kellan raised her blue eyes to meet Orion's leaf-green ones.

"So? Do you agree with him?" There was a long pause as the question hung in the air. "You *do*, don't you?"

"I didn't say that!" Orion shot back.

"But you were thinking it!"

"Oh, the master of the arts arcane has taught you how to reads minds now, has he?"

Kellan started to reply, but Orion cut her off.

"I didn't say anything then because it wasn't the place or time for it." Kellan felt a hot flush rise to her cheeks. He was right about that. She shouldn't have gone off on Lothan in public like that, especially when it came to biz.

"But," Orion continued, raising a hand for emphasis. "I don't necessarily agree with Lothan's attitude. I think he underestimates you, but Lothan underestimates *everyone*, Kellan. He probably can't remember the last time he was involved in a run where he wasn't in charge."

Kellan sighed. "You're probably right. It's just that it's so frustrating."

"I bet. I don't know how you put up with having him as a teacher."

"I have a high tolerance for hardcase instructors," Kellan said with a smile, and Orion glanced down at the sword in his hand, a sheepish expression coming over his face as Kellan laughed.

"It's really not that bad," she explained. "Lothan does know his stuff, and he's taught me a lot. It's just that I don't think he sees I'm already capable of doing more—a lot more. I mean, you've only been working the shadows for a while. You know what I mean."

Orion nodded. "Yeah, it's hard at first when everybody assumes you're going to frag things up. But I think we've both proven we can handle ourselves."

"I want to do more than that. I'm not going to be Lothan's apprentice forever."

"You want to be the one calling the shots," Orion said flatly.

"What's wrong with that?"

"Probably nothing, but you're asking the wrong guy. I'm totally okay with being the hired muscle," he said. "It's what I know how to do. As long as I get paid, I'm better off not worrying about everything else."

"Not me," Kellan said. "I mean, I can follow orders and do what needs to be done, but I don't think I want to do that forever."

"So, what are you going to do about it?"

Kellan sighed again. "I don't know. There's no way Lothan is going to change his mind. . . ."

"Frag Lothan!" Orion shot back. "He's not the only shadowrunner in Seattle. He's not even the only mage, even if he acts like it. You don't need his permission to do some business on your own, right?"

"That's right. I don't."

"So when you see a chance, I say take it."

"Will you back me up if I do?" she asked.

"Assuming you can afford me." Then his serious face split into a grin. "Yeah, of course I'll back you up."

"Thanks."

"Null sheen," the elven adept replied. "So, you ready to go a few more rounds?"

Kellan raised her sword with a nod and assumed a ready pose.

"Let's go," she said. "This time, I'm gonna whip your skinny elf butt."

As it turned out, Orion did most of the butt-whipping, though Kellan managed to get in a few good attacks during their sparring match. She even scored a hit on Orion, and the elf declared himself impressed. He said Kellan was definitely improving. She left the gym bruised, sore and sweaty, but feeling a little better about her altercation with Lothan. It was good to know *someone* thought she had what it took to do things on her own.

Kellan was pleasantly surprised by her growing friendship with Orion, though not as surprised as he was, she suspected. When they first met, she thought Orion was as arrogant in his own way as Lothan, if not more so. He was a member of the Ancients, one of the biggest elven go-gangs in the metroplex. He probably figured her for some nobody newbie shadowrunner. But Kellan's willingness to go out on a limb to pursue the truth, and them working together on two runs back to back had opened the door for them to become friends.

At some point, Kellan had asked Orion to teach her how to use a sword. It was a challenge for both of them. Orion was an adept, endowed with magical talent that made him faster, stronger and more skilled than a mundane swordsman. A lot of his skill with a sword came from his magic, and he wasn't sure it was something he could teach. Kellan had never used any weapon requiring more technique than a stun baton or a pistol. She wasn't sure she even had time to learn how to fence, given how much magical study Lothan loaded onto her. Still, as Orion said, "There are dangers in the Awakened world honest steel can handle better than a gun or shock weapon," and Kellan wanted to be prepared.

There were moments, usually right after Orion gave her a few stinging bruises, when she regretted her decision, but right now she was feeling good about it. Orion was right: she was improving her fencing—just as she was learning more about magic, and about the shadows of Seattle. She was confident she could handle a lot on her own, no matter what Lothan—or the others—thought about her abilities.

It was early in the evening when Kellan got back to her apartment. She trudged wearily up the stairs, listening to the loud argument going on behind the closed door on the second floor as she passed the landing. The ork couple living there was *always* fighting, usually screaming at the top of their lungs. Kellan could only make out about half of what was being said in the patois of English, Spanish and Japanese they called Cityspeak in the Seattle area.

She'd had no place to live when she arrived in Seattle, but she was happy Lothan had not suggested she move in with him. The troll mage valued his privacy too much to share his living quarters, and Kellan wanted her own space. G-Dogg had offered to share his doss, but Kellan turned him down. She definitely didn't want to complicate any of her few professional relationships. She pulled together the cred she needed for a deposit from her cut of her first two runs, and accepted G-Dogg's offer of help in finding a place for her to call her own.

It wasn't much to look at: a small one-bedroom apartment in a run-down building on the edge of the Puyallup Barrens. It was a third-floor walk-up, utilities included, though the water only worked about half the time and her neighbors all had screaming kids who usually played the trideo way too loud— but it was *hers*. Kellan disengaged the maglocks on the door, as always keeping an eye out for anyone unfamiliar in the hallway. She dropped her bag inside and flicked on the light before closing the door and locking it again.

She needed to take a shower and get something to eat, then she'd log on to Shadowland and check out some job possibilities. Shadowland was *the* Matrix host for shadowrunners to exchange information and post leads for biz. Jackie Ozone had set Kellan up with access, and it was the best first step to take in her plan to do something on her own for a change.

First things first, though. She took out her phone and checked her messages. There was only one. *Probably Lothan with more "homework" for me,* she thought as she hit the button to play the message.

"Um, hey, Kellan," a vaguely familiar voice said. "This is Squeak. You probably don't remember me, but I . . . um, I've got something I want to talk to you about, something *big*. Buzz me back, 'kay?" A local telecom grid number appeared at the end of the message. Kellan looked at it thoughtfully as it flashed on the tiny screen.

She actually did remember Squeak. He was a decker, a "warez dood," he called himself. His specialty was hunting through other people's cast-offs, both data and hardware, looking for little nuggets of gold he could turn into cred. Sometimes it was an account number, an old passcode or bits of a deleted file, sometimes it was a piece of tech that could be fixed up and sold. Jackie Ozone bought from him occasionally, and Kellan had met him through Jackie, when the decker was picking up some data for a run not long after Kellan arrived in Seattle. The shy, awkward deckhead had taken a shine to Kellan the moment she'd walked into his squat.

More importantly, from Kellan's perspective, she had made Squeak a standing offer to pay him for any information he might dig up about her mother. Someone had sent Kellan a package from Seattle containing some gear useful for running the shadows, and the dragon-shaped amulet she always wore. The enclosed note said only that the things belonged to her mother. One of the reasons Kellan came to Seattle was to track down the source of the package and find out more about her mother, including whether she was even still alive. Maybe Squeak had a lead.

Kellan punched the button for the phone to dial the highlighted LTG number. It only rang twice before someone answered.

"Hey, Kellan, you get my message?" Squeak asked. Kellan refrained from asking how he knew it was her. She thought the caller ID on her phone was blocked, but apparently not to everyone. That, or the number he gave her was unique, so he would know it was her.

"Yeah, I got it," she replied. "So what's up?"

"Not over the phone," Squeak replied mysteriously. "Can you meet me?" Kellan paused for only a moment. What could Squeak consider to be so important?

"Sure—where and when?"

"How about Syberspace in like . . . an hour?" Squeak was trying to not sound too eager. He wasn't succeeding.

"An hour?" Kellan paused, as if thinking it over. She knew how to avoid sounding too eager, even though she was willing to admit that she was very curious. "All right."

"Wizard! Trust me, Kellan, you won't regret this."

"Okay, Squeak. I'll see you in an hour."

"And Kellan? Come alone," Squeak added before hanging up.

Kellan looked at the phone for a moment, and then hit the END button. Come alone? Squeak had been slotting too many simsense chips. She wondered again what Squeak had found. *Well, there's only one way to find out.* With an hour to get to Syberspace, she had just enough time to catch a quick shower and change into her working clothes.

4

Syberspace, as the name implied, was a club catering to deckers, warez doods, and other tech-heads like Squeak, who were more comfortable in the virtual world of the Matrix than in real life (RL, as the deckers called it). The interior of the club was styled to look like the inside of a Matrix host system, using the widely accepted Universal Matrix Standards. The walls and floor were polished black macroplast, reflecting lights and images in their inky depths. The furniture was all chrome and pure white plastic in simple geometric shapes: tables and chairs cube-shaped or cylindrical, with some white-and-chrome spheres and pyramids scattered around the room as decorations. The pyramids served double duty as terminals for ordering drinks and paying for services via credstick. Multicolored neolux tubing ran along the ceiling and accented the walls, and edged the rails around the main dance floor, where it strobed and flashed in time to the music.

The dance floor itself was the centerpiece of the club. The floor was made up of blocks of translucent plastic, and multicolored lights flashed from below. Supposedly, the lights were programmed in sequences linked to the music. Rumor had it that the flashing lights sometimes transmitted subliminal messages, or caused people to have seizures or hallucinations, but Kellan had never seen evidence of either one.

The club wasn't too busy when she got there. Things wouldn't pick up for at least an hour or two, and that suited Kellan just fine. She was there on business, and the fewer people who noticed, the better. Syberspace wasn't one of her regular hangouts, but she'd been there often enough to know the lay of the land. Her credstick informed the bouncer she was twenty-two rather than nineteen, and he chose not to question her. G-Dogg had made sure Kellan's ID was good enough to pass casual inspection—it was sort of his specialty.

She glanced casually around the club and saw Squeak sitting by himself in a booth near the back, looking a little nervous. He noticed her at the same time, but didn't acknowledge her presence. *Well, at least he's not standing up and waving,* Kellan thought as she made her way over to the table. She slid into the opposite side of the booth.

Squeak probably earned his street name from his

unfortunate resemblance to a nervous rodent. He was small and slightly built, with a pasty complexion that was rarely exposed to the sun. His hair was dirty blond and already beginning to recede from a high forehead, despite the fact he wasn't much older than Kellan. His blue eyes weren't original equipment. They were cybernetic implants, with faint silvery circuit patterns visible in the irises. Unfortunately, getting cybereyes hadn't eliminated Squeak's nervous tendency to glance from side to side, and his implants gave a slight click every time he did, a sound that set Kellan's nerves on edge.

"Hey, Squeak," she said.

"Hoi, Kellan," the warez dood replied with a shy smile and a click of his eyes. "Thanks for coming."

"Null sheen. I hope this is something worth my time."

"Oh, it is," Squeak replied. "It is." The eyes clicked rapidly from side to side as he leaned closer across the table.

"I've got a proposal for a run," he said.

So, it wasn't information about her mother. Kellan was a little disappointed. Still. . . .

"What kind of run?" she asked, keeping her tone carefully neutral.

"A very profitable one," Squeak said. He glanced past her at the club again. *Click-click.* "I was going through some datadumps I collected, you know, mostly trash files and drek like that, seeing if there was anything worth selling off. I found some encrypted files on some old storage media—I'm talking like older than you or me—so I transferred them to my system to see if I could work with them."

"I broke the encryption and recovered some partial e-mail files. The headers said they were United States military communiqués from around the time of the Ghost Dance War."

That piqued Kellan's interest. "Are you sure?" she asked, and Squeak nodded enthusiastically.

"Positive. I triple-checked, and I'm convinced the files are for real."

"What were they about?" Kellan asked. Squeak grinned.

"That's the good part," he said. "The e-mails concerned a United States military stockpile in what is now Salish-Shidhe territory. They were top secret orders to destroy the stockpile before pulling out of the area. From the dates, the orders went out right after the Treaty of Denver was signed and the United States started withdrawing from the Native American Nations."

"So?" Kellan asked. "Where's the run? Those orders went out, what, forty years ago or more. The U.S. troops must have destroyed the stockpile and gotten the frag out of there."

"Yeah, but what if they *didn't?*" Squeak asked. "What if they never got the orders, or they weren't able to carry them out? There are no confirmations in the files, no evidence the orders were actually carried out. There was a lot of drek going down in the

Ghost Dance War, and that part of the country was under NAN control by then. Maybe the U.S. forces didn't get a chance to dispose of all the weapons. What if they're still there?"

"That's a fragging big 'if,' Squeak."

"Yeah, yeah, I know," he said, "but think about it, Kellan!"

"I am," she said. "But even if there are still weapons there, who says they're any good after all this time? They're probably corroded, and besides, they're like forty or fifty years out of date."

"I don't think so," the warez dood replied, his cybereyes clicking in excitement. "This drek was *top secret*, Kellan. It wasn't just racks of assault rifles or grenades or drek like that. We're talking some serious weapons."

"How serious?"

"I don't know," he said. "I couldn't find out from the files, but I'd say something more . . . strategic."

"Stra—" Kellan paused to absorb the implications. "You mean . . . ? Nah. . . ."

Squeak shrugged and shook his head, cutting her off.

"Like I said, I dunno, but think about the *possibilities*."

Kellan's mind was racing with possibilities at that very moment. Squeak was implying the weapons stockpile could contain military grade weapons of mass destruction, most likely chemical or biological, or even tactical nuclear weapons. The old U.S. government certainly had such weapons during that time period, but never deployed them, being unwilling to target the Native American guerrilla forces fighting on their own soil. They were also unwilling to suffer the kind of civilian casualties those weapons would cause.

Though multiple corporate and governmental agreements prohibited the stockpiling of such weapons, it was an open secret in the shadows that governments and megacorporations both had them, in case they were ever needed. If Squeak's information about the weapons cache was good, and there *were* old U.S. military weapons there, the information—and the weapons—would be worth a fortune to the right parties. It would easily net her more nuyen than all the other shadowruns Kellan had done put together, including her runs for Lothan.

"Okay," Kellan said, gathering her thoughts. "Even if there *is* something there after all this time, why me? I mean, if you've got this data, why not just go after those weapons yourself?"

Squeak gave a short, mocking snort. "C'mon, Kellan! I'm a warez dood, not a shadowrunner! My biz is putting together data, writing programs and building hardware, not going on runs. I wouldn't even know how to get *into* the NAN to check this place out."

"So why don't you just sell the data to the NAN or UCAS governments, or someone on Shadowland?"

He shook his head.

"Because I don't know if it's worth anything yet,"

he said. "Besides, if I even hint about what I've got to the Feds or the NAN, then they'll know there's something there. Who's to say they won't just cut me out of the deal, or try to arrest me? No way. But if I've got *proof* or, better yet, if *we* have the weapons . . ."

Then the UCAS and NAN governments, and a few others, would be willing to pay a lot, Kellan concluded silently.

"But first I need someone to check things out," Squeak continued. "That's where you come in."

"And what's in it for me?" Kellan asked.

"A percentage," Squeak said. "I provide the data and we split the profits fifty-fifty."

"All the risk for half the profit?" Kellan said incredulously.

"Not *all* the risk," Squeak protested.

"Most of it. What if it turns out there's nothing there?"

"It's there," Squeak stated positively. "I can feel it, Kellan, but I need your help to confirm it."

"Then I'm going to need more like eighty percent," Kellan said. When it looked like Squeak was going to object, she continued. "If I'm going to put together a team and *pay* them, then I need more."

Squeak thought about it for a moment, but Kellan knew she had him. He didn't know enough other runners to shop around his idea, especially since the more he talked about it, the more likely someone would figure out what he was up to.

"Seventy-five," he offered. Kellan considered for a moment.

"All right."

"Wizard," he said, extending a hand and grinning as Kellan shook it. "When do we get started?"

"Well, if we're doing biz, then I need something to look at so that I can confirm this info is as legit as you think it is," Kellan told him. "I'll get it checked out and get back to you. If I agree that it's good info, I'll put together a team and we can see about making a run."

The warez dood grinned wider and handed her a datachip. "Way ahead of you. I know I'm right.

"Let me buy you a drink. This is the big time, Kellan, I can feel it. We are gonna be fraggin' *rich*."

"You're out of your fraggin' mind, kid," G-Dogg muttered. Kellan looked at Liada, but found no support there. The elf sorceress simply nodded in agreement with G-Dogg's assessment of her proposal.

Kellan had asked the two shadowrunners to meet her at an all-night diner on the outskirts of downtown Seattle. She outlined the general idea of the run, leaving out the details about who had the information and the exact location of the supposed weapons cache. Kellan watched looks of disapproval grow on both their faces as G-Dogg and Liada listened to what she had to say.

"It's way too risky," G-Dogg continued. "You don't know for sure that this swag even exists. Taking an out-of-town run is tricky to begin with, but going into foreign territory just because something *might* be there? Not worth it." He dismissed the idea with a wave of his hand, as if he were cutting all potential ties he might have to it.

"He's right," Liada said, before Kellan could say anything. "It's a waste of time. Anything could have happened in the last forty years. Then there are the border crossings, and actually *finding* whatever it is you're looking for. Besides, if you ask me, some of the drek from the Ghost Dance War is better left buried. Just assume you do find it. How are you going to sell it, and who are you going to sell it to?"

Kellan hadn't really thought that far in advance. Liada was right; finding a buyer for high-grade military weapons wouldn't be easy. There would also be the matter of moving whatever they found out of the NAN and smuggling it into the metroplex, though she supposed she could cut a deal where the buyer moved the goods and she and Squeak split a sizable finder's fee.

"Forget about it, kid," G-Dogg said, noticing her thoughtful look. "This one is just too big."

"Oh, really?" Kellan said, her attention drawn back to the ork. "Is that what you think? That I can't handle the big-time runs?"

"We're just saying don't rush into such a dangerous job on your own, Kellan," Liada said. "You haven't been working the biz in Seattle that long! You've still got a lot to learn. . . ."

47

"I guess so," Kellan retorted. "For example, I thought running the shadows involved taking risks."

"*Justified* risks," G-Dogg said. "You take chances every time you go out the door. The trick is learning what chances are worth taking and what chances aren't—and trust me, this one ain't worth it."

"Fine," Kellan said. She slotted her credstick into the tabletop reader and pushed the key to pay for her share of the tab. Then she stood up to leave, jamming the stick into her pocket.

"Kellan," Liada said, putting a hand on her arm. "Don't take a bad risk just because of what Lothan said. You've got nothing to prove—to him or anyone. You're building a reputation for yourself—"

"Yeah, as Lothan's *apprentice*," she muttered.

"Frag Lothan!" Liada said in a low, fierce voice. "If you're tired of living in his shadow, then find yourself another teacher. But don't go off half-cocked. Promise me you'll at least think twice before you do anything about this run?"

Kellan looked up and saw genuine concern in the elf woman's eyes. Liada had shown before that she truly cared about Kellan's feelings—a rarity in the shadowrunning business. It upset Kellan that Liada couldn't understand how important this run could be to her.

"I'll think about it," she told her friend. "I promise. I gotta get going." She slung her bag over her head, settling it onto her shoulder as she stepped away from the booth. "See you later," she told G-Dogg and Liada.

As she made her way down the street to where she'd parked her Yamaha Rapier, she thought about what her friends had said. *Was* she just doing this because Lothan had hacked her off? She examined that thought for a few minutes, trying to figure out her true motivations. She finally decided that Lothan had just brought to the surface a feeling she already had been struggling with for a while.

She believed she was meant for more than being some old mage's apprentice. She didn't want to spend the rest of her life working the shadows. Lothan had been a shadowrunner since before Kellan was born. If he was so great, why hadn't he hit the big score? Kellan knew why: because he wasn't willing to take the big risks, and it seemed that neither were the runners he worked with. They played it safe, doing little jobs and staying just ahead of the law and their own expenses. When the money started to run out, it was back to another little job.

Kellan couldn't see herself living like that. If she hit the big time, she would have enough cred to set herself up for life, buy herself a new identity and a comfortable life somewhere. Then she'd have the cred to find out what happened to her mother and start a real life for herself, instead of always hustling from one job to another. That was worth a little risk, wasn't it? It was at least worth trying to find out if Squeak's data was solid.

She threw one leg across the seat of her bike and sat there for a minute. Maybe she could talk Squeak into selling the data and cutting her in on a percentage instead of setting up a run. Anyway—when it came to checking out data, Kellan knew who to call.

She took her phone out of her pocket, flipped it open and punched a button. She waited a couple of rings before a female voice answered, "Go."

"Jackie," Kellan said. "We need to talk. I've got some work for you, if you're interested."

Though Kellan had seen Jackie Ozone in person on a few occasions, the decker preferred to meet in the Matrix. So Kellan broke out her new Novatech deck. She sat up comfortably in bed, with pillows propped behind her, and slipped the trode net over her head, adjusting the elastic band so the electrodes rested against the nerve induction points at her temples and brow. Then she powered up the deck, feeling a slight tingle as the diagnostic systems made sure all the connections were up and running. She settled into a comfortable position, looking around to make sure everything was set. Then she punched the GO button on the deck.

There was a moment of disorientation—a sensation of falling, like just before going to sleep. Suddenly, the bedroom of Kellan's apartment was gone, replaced by another room, in another world. It was a small, almost featureless white room, the virtual representation of Kellan's deck. Floating icons represented data files available to her, but Kellan ignored them. Instead, she moved to the "door" of the room. The trode net detected the impulses Kellan's brain sent out, and interpreted them as MOVE commands, directing her virtual persona accordingly.

Outside the little room lay the electronic vista of the Seattle Matrix. A flat black plain stretched off in every direction as far as the eye could see. Kellan's private room was nothing more than a meter-high white pyramid at her feet (the feet of her virtual self, that is). Glowing lines of data stretched off in every direction. The icons of other systems and hosts were visible in the distance. Kellan saw the familiar sights of the Mitsuhama Pagoda, the Aztechnology Pyramid (looking much like its real-world self) and the Novatech Star, giants dominating the virtual skyline. Smaller systems clustered around, making the Matrix look like a fantastic city, where the only limits on construction were imagination and the Universal Matrix Standards, which dictated how certain things looked and felt in cyberspace.

Kellan stepped away from the white pyramid onto a dataline. There was a rush of motion as she surged down the line, glowing packets of data whizzing past her, the virtual landscape nothing but a blur. Kellan felt several rapid changes in direction, but the simsense safeguards kept her from feeling nauseous or disoriented.

In an instant, she found herself standing beside another nondescript white pyramid representing another host system. The only way she knew she had moved at all was the change in perspective. The skyline was different here.

There was no sculpting to call attention to the host system, nothing making it any different from thousands of other minor systems and access points in the Matrix. Kellan knew that if she wished, she could superimpose an LTG code over the pyramid—its "address" in cyberspace—but there was no need. She already knew "where" it was, and what it was. She took a step forward and entered.

Her cyberdeck and the host system carried out a complex dance, exchanging passcodes and information, so quickly Kellan wasn't even aware of the process. The host system verified her identity, and she suddenly found herself at the entrance to a bar. If the host computer had *not* approved her ID, she would have found herself somewhere considerably less pleasant. She'd heard stories about the shadow-cells, and the stories alone were enough to convince her to avoid them at all costs. Deckers talked about existing in a complete void, an eternity of nothingness: blind, deaf and adrift in endless darkness, unable to jack out of the Matrix. Exile to a shadowcell usually lasted for only for a few minutes, but it *seemed* like an eternity, and there were stories of people whose minds never really came back. The sysops of Shadowland took their security seriously. They had to, considering that their clientele consisted primarily of shadowrunners, who guarded their privacy as jealously as any corp.

The virtual bar was one of several on Shadowland's host system. Its design showed off the programming skill of its creators: perfect in nearly every detail. The floors were polished black marble, shot through with veins of white and silver, as was the top of the curved bar. The furniture was all dark-stained wood, black leather and chrome accents. The tabletops were cool, smoky glass. Kellan could hear the click of her virtual footsteps on the tiles, feel the cool air on her nonexistent skin, and even see her reflection distorted in the chrome and the polished marble. She heard the clinking of ice in glasses and smelled exotic liqueurs and perfumes.

The bar's clientele presented a stark contrast to the decor's sharply drawn realism. It was like walking in on a convention of cartoons, faerie tales, figments, dreams and nightmares. At the moment Kellan walked in, the bar patrons included a sinuous Asian dragon, coiled into a wing chair and sipping tea from a delicate china cup. He was chatting with a white rabbit in a red velvet jacket and paisley waistcoat adorned with a gold watch fob. There was a figure in black medieval armor, face obscured by a hooded cloak, only a pair of burning red eyes showing where his face should be. Gossamer-winged faeries chatted up sexy chrome robots, bizarre aliens talked to famous people from history and popular characters from fiction, from Abe Lincoln to some *chica* Kellan vaguely recognized from old rock vids. There was a constant buzz of background conversation, but privacy protocols kept everyone in the bar from overhearing anything they shouldn't (unless they had the chops to circumvent the protocols).

She spotted Jackie waiting for her at a table. The decker's persona looked like a young girl from a Japanese-inspired cartoon, complete with wide eyes, tiny mouth and a flowing white dress. A wide headband held back her black hair and she waved as Kellan approached.

"We've got to do something about getting you a better persona," she said by way of a greeting, and Kellan suddenly felt self-conscious. Her own icon was an off-the-shelf persona, customized to look vaguely like her real self—medium-length brown hair, medium height, slender build—but low-resolution and crude compared to the other characters in the bar. She knew that in a place like Shadowland it marked her as a non-decker, or someone who didn't have the connections to get the best software. It certainly wasn't the impression she wanted to make, but she didn't frequent Shadowland's virtual rooms often enough to want to shell out the nuyen for anything better. She usually read and posted on the system's message boards, where your persona didn't matter.

"Don't worry," Jackie continued, sensing Kellan's unease (impressive, considering Kellan's persona wasn't sophisticated enough to reflect her feelings). "I can set you up with something."

"Thanks."

"But you probably didn't come here to talk about updating your software," Jackie offered.

"Nope, I've got business."

Jackie's persona favored her with a bright smile. "One of my favorite words. I'm all ears." Settling her chin on the heels of both hands, she leaned forward, elbows on the table, big eyes looking expectantly at Kellan.

Kellan felt that Jackie was more receptive to her proposal than Liada and G-Dogg had been, though it was hard to tell if the decker was taking her seriously. On the other hand, it was sometimes hard to tell if Jackie took *anything* seriously. Kellan explained about the information she had gotten from Squeak, and Jackie listened carefully, clearly grasping its potential value.

"I can do some research for you," the decker offered when Kellan finished, "but it sounds to me like you're not going to need a decker where you're going."

"We might," Kellan replied. "There could be electronic security . . . " but Jackie cut her off with a shake of her head.

"Electronic security that's not connected to the Matrix," she pointed out. "Whatever you're going to be dealing with is out there somewhere," she gestured off vaguely into space, indicating the real world beyond the virtual reality they occupied. "That's not my area. I'll do the research, but once you get outside the metroplex, you're going to be on your own."

Kellan nodded her agreement.

"Okay," she replied. "I understand. How much for . . . ?"

Jackie waved one hand in a dismissive gesture, shaking her head. "Your cred's no good here, kid. I'll do this for you as a favor. If it gets complicated, we can talk compensation, but for now let's see what I can dig up, okay?"

"No," Kellan said, "I'll pay. . . ."

The decker laughed. "Really, don't worry about it. You couldn't afford me otherwise." When Kellan tried again to object, Jackie continued. "It's null sheen, just some background checks. I don't mind doing it."

Kellan smiled. "Thanks, Jackie, I appreciate it."

"No problem," the decker said. "Just give me what you've got and I'll get on it."

Kellan fished in the pocket of the jacket her persona wore and took out a small black card, about the size of a business card, which she held out to Jackie. The decker's persona plucked it from her hand, triggering the transfer of data from Kellan's system to hers. By the time Jackie slipped the card out of sight, the transfer was complete.

"I'll let you know as soon as I've got something," she told Kellan.

"Okay. And thanks again, Jackie."

"Null sheen," the decker replied. "Take care."

Kellan made a point of leaving the virtual bar before logging off the Matrix. Jackie had taught her that it was poor form to simply vanish from a virtual meeting place. She opened her eyes to the familiar surroundings of her bedroom, pulling off the trode net and setting aside the cyberdeck. She leaned back against the pillows with a sigh. There was nothing to do now but wait until Jackie contacted her with the results of her research into Squeak's data. Then she could decide whether there was a potential run in it or not. Thinking about how interested Jackie seemed in what she'd had to say, Kellan hoped that interest meant good news.

She began reviewing the text on conjuring that Lothan had asked her to read before their next lesson, but her heart really wasn't in it. All she could think about was her next meeting with Squeak and what his data might turn up. She finally fell asleep, the datapad lying on her stomach, dreaming about Lothan being struck speechless when she showed off the results of her successful shadowrun—a run she accomplished without any help from him at all.

5

Kellan normally looked forward to her magic lessons with Lothan. Like most of the rest of the world, she found him hard to take at times, but the troll mage definitely knew his stuff. He was also a surprisingly good teacher—at least, Kellan learned quickly under his tutelage. Though Lothan rarely praised her work, he still managed to make it clear that Kellan's magical training was advancing quickly and well. Naturally, he took most of the credit for the development of her talent, but knowing she was improving so dramatically still made Kellan feel good.

Today, however, Kellan wished she was anywhere other than Lothan's dim, crowded study. All her focus was on the potential run she had in the works, and certainly not on the current arcane topic on which Lothan chose to expound. She just wanted to get the lesson over with so she could meet with

Squeak. What was worse, Lothan had chosen today to begin teaching Kellan more about conjuring and spirits, two topics Kellan just couldn't seem to grasp. Though her spellcasting abilities had developed considerably and she was getting the hang of astral work, Kellan had a difficult time with conjury. No matter how many texts she read on the subject, it just didn't click for her.

The fact that Lothan's renewed interest in teaching her conjuring seemed to be a direct result of her interrupting his banishing spell on their recent run didn't make Kellan feel any better. Though he didn't say so in plain words, it was clear the old troll felt Kellan's handling of the air elemental outside the Aztechnology Pyramid was less than elegant. He wanted to teach her the "proper" way of dealing with spirits. *Seems like blasting them works just fine,* Kellan thought glumly. Still, she tried to pay attention to Lothan's explanation.

"So," he concluded, drawing to a close a long exposition, "once the ritual is complete, the spirit appears in the ethereal plane at the behest of the conjurer, where it is bound by the ritual and the power of the diagrams and forced to obey its new master. It is then ready to be commanded into service."

Kellan leaned forward on the red velvet settee, gesturing with the datapad in her hand.

"But where does the spirit come from?" she asked. "The metaplanes?"

"That is the most commonly accepted theory," Lothan replied, turning away from the flatscreen display showing various hermetic diagrams used for conjuring.

"Isn't that a bit like slavery, then, snatching a spirit away from its home and forcing it to do what you want?"

"Nonsense," the troll snorted. "It's nothing of the sort. Elementals are formed from the energies of the metaplanes, channeled by the conjuring rituals and given form by the will of their summoner."

"That's one *theory*," Kellan countered, waving the datapad for emphasis. "But the O'Neill hypothesis says elementals have an independent existence before they are summoned to this plane, and Dr. White-Eagle speculated about elemental oversouls and a greater consciousness of the elemental metaplanes."

Lothan raised one shaggy gray eyebrow, a faint smile creasing the corners of his mouth. "Well, you *have* been doing the reading, haven't you? All right, then," he said, "do you have a moral objection to the rites of conjuring, then?"

"Not a *moral* objection," Kellan said slowly, searching for words. "It's just . . . well, don't you think if elementals *do* have free will, they would get pretty hacked off at being called up and bossed around all the time?"

"If that's true, no elemental has ever said anything about it to me," Lothan replied with a smug expression.

"Well, maybe they *can't*, or they're afraid to . . ."

Kellan began, and then she threw Lothan a disgusted look. "You aren't even taking this seriously, are you?"

"Of course I am, my dear," the mage replied. "I'm very pleased that you've considered some alternate points of view, however erroneous they may be."

"So you don't think spirits are real?"

"That depends entirely upon how you define 'spirits' and 'real'," Lothan replied. "Do spirits exist? Unquestionably. We can see their effects and interact with them. Are spirits intelligent? Again, without a doubt. Many spirits are capable of carrying out complex instructions and even reasoning to a degree. Free spirits have shown considerable intelligence and cunning. Is summoning and binding elementals slavery? Hardly."

As Kellan opened her mouth to protest, Lothan raised a finger to indicate he wasn't finished. "Consider computers. There are programs so sophisticated you would swear they were intelligent, capable of adapting to their circumstances and interacting with living people. But you wouldn't claim one of these programs was truly conscious or 'alive'."

"There are rumors—" Kellan began.

"Yes, yes," Lothan countered with a dismissive wave. "There are rumors of artificial intelligences secretly roaming the depths of the Matrix, hidden from the outside world. I've heard them all before, and I've still never seen any proof of these elusive, so-called AIs."

"Just because you haven't seen one doesn't mean they don't exist," Kellan said stubbornly.

"An ideally unprovable supposition. Do you think the difficulties you've been having with conjuring stem from your concerns about hurting the spirits' feelings?" The edge of mockery in Lothan's tone made Kellan clench her jaw.

"No," she said. "Maybe . . . I don't know." She gestured vaguely and slumped back on the settee, dropping the datapad into her lap.

Lothan stroked his chin for a moment with one big hand. "Perhaps it's time for a more practical demonstration," he said, rising to his feet. "Come."

Kellan followed as Lothan led her from the study to a door she hadn't entered before. Beyond the door, wooden stairs led down into the basement. Lothan squeezed his large frame through the doorway, ducking his head. Kellan followed him down the stairs into darkness.

"Close the door," Lothan said, and Kellan complied, shutting out the light coming from upstairs. Candles suddenly sprang to life in the basement below, casting a rich, golden glow. Kellan reached the foot of the stairs and took in the contents of the room before her.

"Wizard," she breathed.

The basement room was larger than she'd expected. It had to run the entire length of the house. Part of it was walled off—that side of the room most likely containing the furnace, water heater and other appliances. The rest was one large room. The walls were paneled in dark wood, and the floor was concrete.

The entire room was set up as a magical workshop. Tall workbenches extended along two walls. Their surfaces were covered with beakers and flasks of dark and intensely colored liquids, rolls of parchment and stacks of loosely bound paper. Notebooks and ring binders stood at the end of one bench between heavy brass bookends. On the walls above the benches hung shelves that continued up to the ceiling, holding even more mystical miscellany. Jars of dried herbs—and other things Kellan couldn't identify by sight—crowded one set of shelves. Another held incense, charcoal, censers, crystals and a rainbow of colored chalk.

The most impressive thing about the room however, was what was on the floor. A complex diagram was drawn on the smooth concrete in colored chalk, nearly filling the entire room. It was a circle, four meters in diameter. Inside the outer circle were several smaller concentric circles. Magical symbols filled the spaces in between the bands, running all around the circle. Inside those was a six-pointed star formed by two overlapping triangles. Within the star was another circle, edged in still more arcane symbols. Symbols were also inscribed within each segment of the star's points and at the points themselves. Candles were held to the floor by melted wax at five points of the star. At the sixth point stood a brass tripod and brazier, together measuring a little more than a meter high.

"A summoning circle?" Kellan asked, and Lothan nodded.

"Quite so. Now I shall demonstrate exactly *how* it is used," he replied. He pointed to a stool near one of the workbenches. "Set that in a corner, outside the circle, and watch very carefully. I want you to pay close attention to the flow of energies. Do *not*, under any circumstances, interrupt the ritual once it has begun or disturb any part of the circle. Do you understand?"

Kellan nodded in reply, moving to fetch the stool.

"Good," Lothan said. "You can help me gather the materials I'll need."

Kellan helped Lothan choose ingredients from jars and containers on the shelves: sulphur, frankincense, copal resin and other pungent herbs. These Lothan mixed together in a great wooden mortar, grinding them into a fine powder. Then he took a smaller jar and added several pinches of gold dust, before picking up another jar and twisting off the lid.

"Powdered ruby," the mage said as he shook sparkling reddish dust into the mortar. This was mixed with the rest of the ingredients.

"The brazier, if you would be so kind," Lothan requested, and Kellan walked around the outside of the circle. The brass brazier was already neatly stacked with charcoal. Closing her eyes and taking a deep breath, Kellan passed her hand over the pan.

She concentrated for a moment. When she opened her eyes, the charcoal was beginning to glow red around the edges. When she lowered her hand to her side a few moments later, there was a bright, cherry-red glow at the heart of the stack, giving off a warmth that suffused the room.

"Well done. No explosions this time," Lothan muttered. Kellan was about to make a comment when her teacher stepped into the conjuring circle, placing the mortar at the base of the brazier.

"Very good. You can take your seat now," he said. "Make sure your phone is off, and that there won't be any other distractions." Kellan took the phone from her pocket and set it to take messages. Then she hopped back up on the stool and watched Lothan work.

The mage extinguished most of the candles in the basement room, until there was so little light that Kellan thought Lothan must be working from memory rather than by sight. Then he stepped into the middle of the conjuring circle and stood facing the brazier. He dropped a pinch of the mixture from the mortar onto the hot coals. A thin stream of pungent, sweet-smelling smoke rose up.

Turning clockwise, Lothan faced in turn each of the five candles at the points of the star. He recited words in a language foreign to Kellan and traced symbols in the air above each candle. To Kellan's astral sight, the symbols faintly glowed. She recognized the symbols as representing the elements—

earth, air, fire, water and spirit. As Lothan completed each symbol above a candle, a flame sprang to life, shedding a golden glow over the circle.

Three times Lothan went around the circle. When the circuits were complete, Kellan became aware that a shimmering translucent dome separated her from her teacher. Its outer edge exactly followed the circumference of the circle. It extended up over Lothan's head, brushing the ceiling at its apex. From Kellan's point of view, everything inside the dome was slightly distorted, like she was looking through thick glass. She knew that the dome was a ward activated by Lothan's ritual to help shield the mage from astral interference during the summoning ritual. Kellan was *outside* the ward, and she knew it also was intended to help contain the energies of the ritual and protect bystanders.

Lothan dropped more incense onto the coals. The ward seemed to contain most of the smoke, but not all of it. The slight haze inside the dome gave things a dreamlike quality. Lothan planted his feet firmly, squared his shoulders and raised his hands as he began chanting. Kellan felt a tingle wash over her, the first ripples of Lothan's summoning ritual. She watched as the troll mage slowly built up magical energy inside the shimmering ward.

The chanting rose and fell. The rest of the incense went into the brazier, little by little, along with wood chips and shavings: rowan, apple, oak and holly. The tang of smoke filled the basement. The coals of the fire glowed red-hot as it crackled and snapped. Kellan sweated, sitting as still as possible and watching carefully. The rite seemed to go on forever. Then Lothan spread his arms wide, out to the edges of the circle.

"By the power of earth, I compel you!
By the power of air, I compel you!
By the power of water, I compel you!
By the power of fire eternal, I compel you!
I conjure and charge thee, oh spirit of fire, arise!
Arise at my command and truly do my will!"

Kellan felt the murmur of power surge into a rushing crescendo.

"Arise!" Lothan commanded again, and there was a flash of fire from the brazier that made Kellan jump. A puff of flame shot up from the coals into the smoke-filled air. It hung there, hovering about half a meter above the brazier. The fire seemed to condense into a small, glowing shape surrounded by a shimmer of heat and a corona of light the size of a beach ball. The warmth it was throwing off made Kellan sweat even more, but Lothan appeared cool and comfortable.

The troll mage turned his palms to the floor, and slowly lowered his arms. The dome of the ward lowered along with them. When Lothan's arms reached his sides, the ward was gone. Only the hovering fire elemental remained. Kellan saw it clearly now; it looked like a large lizard, maybe half a meter in length. Its scales were deep red fading to orange along its belly, and its eyes glowed like hot coals.

"There." Lothan gestured toward the spirit with a theatrical wave of one hand. "Here we have a simple fire elemental—a salamander, as it is commonly known." The spirit shifted and lashed its tail, but otherwise hovered right where it was, close by Lothan.

"Did watching the summoning help you understand what is required?" he asked Kellan.

"I watched really closely," she said, shifting her eyes away from the elemental and back to Lothan. "But I still don't see how you did it. I mean, what part of the chanting actually called the spirit?"

Lothan gave a tired sigh. With a negligent wave of one hand, he dismissed the elemental. It faded and then winked out like a candle deprived of oxygen, disappearing into the smoky air, which immediately felt cooler.

"As with sorcery, it is not the precise words you use that matter," the troll said patiently, stepping out of the circle to crack open a window and let in some fresh air. "It's your intent and focus. The chanting, the gestures and so forth merely provide a means of attaining that focus."

Kellan nodded, and Lothan continued.

"The key is to gather in power, then project it with the intent of bringing the spirit into being and binding it to your will." Seeing the look on Kellan's face, Lothan gave a lopsided smile and raised a shaggy eyebrow. "Ah, there's the concern over elemental servitude again," he said.

Kellan shrugged. "What if you *don't* focus on binding it?" she asked.

"Then the spirit is free to do as it wishes in the world. Do you know what the first act of an uncontrolled spirit typically is?"

Kellan shook her head.

"To slay its summoner," Lothan continued. He snapped his fingers suddenly for emphasis, and the sound made Kellan start. "A spirit's summoner has a degree of power over it, whether it is controlled or not. So a spirit that escapes service will take measures to ensure it is never controlled again."

"Can't say I blame it," Kellan muttered, and Lothan sighed again.

"I can see we'll get nowhere with this discussion today," he said, picking up a brass lid and capping the smoldering brazier. "If you don't want to learn the art of conjuring, please—"

"I do," Kellan interrupted. "It's just that—"

Lothan broke into her thought. "We'll pick this up another time. I think we've both had enough for one day. Do some further reading on the subject, and perhaps try some conjuring on your own. Focus on the material about watchers; there are far fewer consequences for failing to properly summon such a low-powered spirit. Then, if you decide you want to pursue conjuring, I will endeavor to teach it. If not, we will move on. Fair?"

Kellan agreed. She helped put away the materials from the ritual and cleaned up the room before leaving. It wasn't until she left the house that she realized she'd forgotten to turn her phone back on. She checked and found she had a message from Jackie.

"Hoi, Kellan," the decker said, "I checked out the data you gave me and I've got to say it doesn't look good. Some of my contacts say the U.S. military was very efficient about dealing with those old weapons depots, and the NAN has been over that area lots of times in the past forty years. Odds are the intel you got is way out of date. If you ask me—and you did— I wouldn't bother running with it. Sorry."

Kellan punched the command to delete the message, then hit the END button. *Well, so much for the big score*, she thought sourly. She considered calling Jackie back, but what would be the point? Jackie would just repeat what she'd said in her message, and Kellan really didn't want to hear it a second time. *I should call Squeak and tell him it's a no-go.* She scrolled to his number on her phone, finger resting on the CALL button. Then she closed the phone and slipped it back into her pocket. *No*, she decided, thinking about what G-Dogg had taught her about dealing with other shadowrunners, *this is business I should handle in person.*

6

Jackie Ozone preferred the virtual world. In her opinion, the Matrix was better than the real world: cleaner, faster, with rules that made sense. Still, Jackie wasn't one of those deckheads who wanted nothing more than an IV hookup and a comfortable bed that would let her stay jacked in for days on end. She acknowledged the real world, and lived in it. She just preferred doing business online, where she felt secure. This meeting, however, would take place in person, which was how her client wanted it. For Jackie, closing the deal always won out over her personal preferences.

In fact, closing the deal won out over *everything*, as far as Jackie Ozone was concerned. She was in the shadows to make money, and she did whatever it took to bring in the nuyen. So now she waited patiently at the small coffee shop in downtown Seattle, one of hundreds of its sort in the metroplex. She'd ordered a small soylatte, but had barely touched it. With her pocket secretary in hand, her stylish clothes and the chrome of her datajack gleaming from her right temple, Jackie looked like an up-and-coming young corporate exec, or an in-demand contract worker. It was a carefully constructed image.

She sat and ignored her drink for only a few minutes before the door of the shop opened and another smartly dressed woman entered. She made her way directly to Jackie's table.

"Jackie," the woman said by way of greeting. Her blond hair was straight and stylish, cut precisely long enough to brush her jaw and frame her finely chiseled face. Sunglasses covered her eyes and accented her pale skin. A dark blue pantsuit flattered the toned curves of her body. She was store-bought perfection in every way.

"Eve," Jackie replied, gesturing toward the empty chair on the opposite side of the table. "Right on time."

"Well, you said it was something worthwhile." Eve slid into the seat, setting her shoulder bag on the floor beside her. She didn't take off her glasses. She apparently had no qualms about sitting with her back to the door.

"Oh, I'm very confident you'll like this," Jackie assured her. She laid her pocket secretary on the table and spun it so that it faced the other woman. Eve picked it up and touched the screen to activate it, scrolling down a few times to read the entire file.

Jackie couldn't see her eyes, but she thought she saw the faintest flicker of a raised eyebrow.

"Can this be legit?" Eve asked the decker, placing the palmtop on the table. Her tone hadn't changed, but her question betrayed her interest.

"Everything I've been able to access tells me that there's a very good chance something is still there."

"It's been a long time," Eve countered.

"Half a century's not that long for the kind of materiel we're talking about, especially if parts of the facility were sealed." Jackie could feel the other woman's ambivalence. "The kicker," she added casually, "is that Ares was supposed to oversee the decommissioning and disposal of the contents for a lot of sites like this one, but for this particular location, I can find no records of that ever happening."

"Interesting. What if Ares did the job but just covered it up, or the records were lost, or stolen?"

Jackie shook her head. "I don't think so. More likely Ares pocketed the money from the U.S. government and then access to the site fell through after the Treaty of Denver, or because of some other trouble. It was easier to just ignore the problem, especially since it was in foreign territory."

"Where did you get this information?" Eve asked, slowly spinning the palmtop on the table. She seemed to be considering the value of the intel. "Who else knows about it?"

Jackie had expected this question. Without missing a beat, she answered, "Some warez dood." She didn't

mention Kellan's part. It was better for everyone—
especially Kellan—if she stayed out of this.

"Does he know what he's got?"

"He must have some idea, but he's strictly small-
time."

"You have the rest of this?" Eve asked, holding
out the pocket secretary. Jackie took it.

"Of course. If I didn't, I wouldn't have called."

Eve favored her with a slight smile.

"All right, then," she said. "If you say it's legit, I
can think of several uses for it—one in particular
comes to mind. It's an angle we've been cultivating
for a while."

"A run?"

Her contact shook her head.

"No, an . . . interested party. If you're willing to
deliver the data, I'll arrange for double your usual
finder's fee."

"Deliver it where?" Jackie asked. She didn't much
care for the way Eve smiled in return.

Telling Kellan her data was worthless was not even
close to the worst thing Jackie ever did to a fellow
runner. By the time she met with Eve, the decker had
convinced herself it was for Kellan's own good. The
kid was too green to handle a run like this, anyway.
Better she let the professionals handle it than run off
and get herself killed.

After concluding her deal with Eve, Jackie had to
admit she was having second thoughts. Not about

selling the data, but about agreeing to deliver it to her contact's "interested party." To her, that phrase usually meant some shadowrunner specializing in salvage operations—maybe an arms dealer or a fixer with good connections. Jackie knew her share of that type of person, and had no problem dealing with them. Under normal circumstances, she would secure the data in storage somewhere online, then provide access once payment was delivered to an untraceable account. But the interested party wanted it delivered in person, to a physical location. And once Jackie found out where, it was obvious why.

They called it the Rat's Nest, and with good reason. It was part of the Redmond Barrens. Officially, it was the North Seattle Refuse Center, a huge open-air landfill north of the Snoqualmie River on the edge of Salish-Shidhe territory. Unofficially, the Rat's Nest was home to the human and metahuman refuse of society. Hundreds of squatters inhabited the maze-like mounds of trash, scratching out a living scavenging everything useful from the landfill. They built tents and lean-to huts from packing material, plastic tarps and other found materials, and the homes—and their inhabitants— blended into the landscape of garbage. The stench made Jackie glad she'd worn a breather mask, which filtered out the worst of it.

Eve said her client preferred doing biz at night, but there was no way Jackie was visiting the Rat's Nest after dark. She agreed to a meet at sunset, figuring that was as close to daytime as she was going to get, and as close to night as she was willing to go. So, as the setting sun lit up the chemically tinged sky in a spectacular palette of colors, Jackie picked her way past the trash-laden paths just inside the entrance to the landfill. The underpaid guards employed by the metroplex ignored her. Their job was primarily to make sure that what was inside the Rat's Nest *stayed* inside—one more poor fragger going in was no concern of theirs.

She'd been assured safe passage, but Jackie felt the weight of what she was sure were hundreds of eyes watching her, concealed in the ragged tents and shadowy piles of refuse. Her hand closed around the light automatic pistol she carried in her shoulder bag. The Rat's Nest was well named, and its inhabitants weren't just human or metahuman. She'd read stories about the devil rats, hideous paranormal creatures the size of small dogs, and the other dangerous creatures lurking in the mounds of trash.

Her directions to the meet site were solid, and she found it without a single wrong turn. A strange sort of totem pole, like an idol built by a tribe worshipping the cast-offs of modern society, thrust up out of a mound of garbage that nearly hid the door to a warehouse. The totem pole incorporated several broken trideo sets, meters of fiber-optic cable, keyboards and other computer peripherals, and a stained store mannequin with no legs. Jackie stared at it, mesmerized with a strange sort of fascination. The feeling of being watched intensified as she stood in front of the totem pole, and she forced herself to slow her breathing, trying to show no outward signs of concern.

Where the frag is he? she wondered frantically.

As if summoned by her thought, a shadow detached from the mound behind the totem and glided toward her. Jackie turned as the figure stepped into the fading light that spilled through the gap between the putrid hills.

He was human, most likely. It was difficult to tell because his flesh was so heavily scarred, pierced and decorated. Staples ran along his bald scalp and across one cheek, stretching taut his leathery skin, with heavy chrome rings piercing brow and cheek. It was as if his face were a mask of flayed skin worn over muscle and bone. A dark beard stubble was visible in spots, but otherwise his eyebrows were the only hair on his face. His eyes were pits of shadow beneath those dark brows, but Jackie thought wildly that she saw a gleam of red where his eyes should be.

His clothing was a mismatched collection of synthleathers that creaked slightly as he moved. A padded biker's vest and pants were topped by heavy shin guards, vambraces and shoulder pads. Jackie recognized some of the equipment as parts of a sports uniform of some sort, probably combat biker or urban brawl. Draped across his back like a cloak was a plastic slicker, coated to repel acid rain. Fingerless synthleather gauntlets creaked as he flexed his hands, which appeared empty.

"Zhade?" Jackie asked in a cautious tone, never taking her hand off the gun in her bag. The figure nodded.

"You have the goods?" he asked, his voice the rasp of a lifelong smoker, or someone forced to breathe smog-laden air for too long.

"Yes," she said.

"Leave it and go." As he spoke, Jackie caught a flicker of movement from beside the totem pole. A bulbous, gray-furred shape shuffled out of the shadows, beady red eyes gleaming in the fading, blood-red sunlight, whiskers twitching as it sniffed the air. The creature was not quite a meter in length. Zhade showed no concern at its arrival.

Jackie reached slowly into the inside pocket of her jacket with her free hand and withdrew a datapad containing all the information she'd gathered. When she moved, the devil rat scampered to where Zhade stood and curled around his feet like a well-heeled dog, crouching down on all fours and watching her every move.

She held up the datapad so Zhade could see it, then laid it on the ground at her feet.

"It's all there," she said. Then she took a step backward, keeping her eyes on the devil rat. She could hear scrabbling and scratching from the surrounding trash.

She continued walking backward until Zhade and his pet were out of sight around the edge of the mound. Then she turned and strode purposefully back toward the entrance. She forced herself not to look toward any of the faint noises coming from either side, and not to run. Her hand clutched her pistol so hard that her fingers hurt. The landfill guards looked at her curiously when she walked out, but didn't try to stop her. It wasn't until Jackie had driven a couple of kilometers away from the Rat's Nest that she pulled over to the side of the road to take a few long, deep breaths. She rested her forehead against the steering wheel for a moment before resolutely straightening up in her seat.

"Toxic," she said under her breath, thinking of Zhade, the totem of refuse, the devil rats. A toxic Rat shaman. She'd never encountered one before, but you didn't work in the shadows for long without hearing rumors and stories. She had long assumed that toxic shamans were real. Shamans drew their magical power from the natural world, from a relationship with their totem spirits. It made a twisted kind of sense, then, that toxic shamans found power in everything *un*natural, in garbage and pollution, waste and filth. Those same stories also said toxic shamans were all deranged, unhinged by contact with magical powers no one could deal with and stay sane. Zhade certainly fit the profile. The look in his eyes . . .

Jackie gripped the steering wheel. It was over and done with. She would check the proper account when she got home to confirm the transfer of funds. Otherwise, her part in the deal was done. She was looking forward to a long bath, and forgetting every-thing about the Rat's Nest and what lurked there. But as she put the car into gear and eased it back onto the road, she couldn't help wondering: what kind of ties did Eve's organization have to a freak like Zhade?

She wouldn't even let herself think about the kind of "salvage" he would be interested in—or what he'd do with it.

7

Squeak lived in Redmond, so it took Kellan a while to get there from Lothan's place on Capitol Hill. Lots of warez doods and deckheads like Squeak lived in the Redmond Barrens, filled as it was with buildings wired for telecommunications, with old fiber-optic trunk lines and jackpoints scattered everywhere. Pirate deckers and techies found plenty of places to access the virtual world and carry out their business.

High-priced deckers like Jackie Ozone didn't live in Redmond, but the combination of Matrix accessibility and cheap (read: usually free) real estate made it attractive to minor-leaguers like Squeak. You just had to be willing to live with the gangs, the scavengers, the squatters and the complete lack of any metroplex services, including police. It was the life of a lot of people in the shadows.

As Kellan crossed Lake Washington, she toyed

with half-formed ideas for explaining the situation to Squeak. Afterward, she figured she'd drown her sorrows at one of the local watering holes. Squeak's place was close to Touristville, on the border between Redmond and Bellevue. It was where the straight citizens came to experience life on the edge, a night of "slumming in the Barrens." Redmond's most successful clubs and bars were located there, along with the denizens who could afford to live in this "upscale" area. People knew Kellan's face in some of those clubs, but she was confident that she'd be able to avoid any unwanted company.

The area around Touristville was Brain Eater turf. Even if Kellan didn't already know it, graffiti proclaimed it to everyone who wasn't legally blind. BRAIN EATERS RULE! and other such brilliant slogans were splashed across buildings and fences, along with the gang's red-fez-and-green-brain logo. The Brain Eaters were techies, scavengers and warez doods like Squeak. In fact, Kellan assumed Squeak was a member of a gang, or had been at one time. Like her, he was probably counting on this being his big break, his chance of getting out of the gang and the Barrens. Kellan hated to be the one to disappoint him.

She parked her bike in the alley beside the rundown apartment building, engaging the security system as she dismounted. It would set up a hell of a racket if anyone touched the bike. People in the Barrens ignored vehicle alarms, of course, but at least

Kellan would know before she left the building that someone had fragged with her ride—or tried to. She looked up at the side of the graffiti-encrusted building and the rusting iron latticework of the fire escapes looming overhead. Once, the place was probably pretty nice, decent apartments for corporate employees working in the district. Since the Crash, it had clearly deteriorated. Most such places were now owned by metroplex slumlords. They squeezed out extra profit by refusing to pay for maintenance, taking full advantage of the fact that most of their tenants didn't even legally exist. It wasn't like metroplex health and safety inspectors came out to the Barrens.

Kellan took the front steps two at a time and stepped into the building's small, dimly lit foyer. The smell of mildew and rotting carpet assaulted her nose as she hunted on the panel for Squeak's apartment number. She hit the buzzer and waited. There was no response.

Damn, Kellan thought. She knew she'd been taking a chance that he wouldn't be home when she decided not to call first. But Squeak struck her as someone who didn't get out much, so she'd figured it was a gamble with better than even odds. She hit the buzzer again and waited. Still nothing.

Maybe he's jacked in. If that was the case, he'd barely be aware of the real world at all. He sure wouldn't hear the buzzer. *Maybe I should have just called.* But Kellan wanted to do this face-to-face— maybe she could call Squeak and find out where he was, and just leave a message and be done with it if he didn't answer. *Then at least I'd have given it my best shot.*

As Kellan reached for her cell phone, an ork woman came down the inside stairs. She was spilling out of a lime green tank top and pair of shiny black neospandex pants, her hair dyed a brilliant red, and gelled and moussed to within a centimeter of its life. She pushed open the door and passed Kellan with a sidelong glance. Kellan caught the inner door before it closed and stepped inside.

She headed up the stairs. Maybe, if Squeak was home, she could get his attention. If not, then she would call and leave him a message and tell him no deal. She climbed up to the third-floor landing and scanned the hallway. The carpet was worn and the lights dim—low-wattage bulbs, compounded by damage to some of the fixtures. All the apartment doors were closed, but Kellan could still hear pounding music and voices shouting in Cityspeak as she walked past.

She stopped at Squeak's door and rapped firmly. The door swung inward slightly when she knocked, and Kellan involuntarily took a step back. There was no light inside the apartment. Kellan didn't have a good feeling about this. Glancing up and down the hall to make sure it was empty, she reached into her jacket and withdrew her Ares Crusader machine pistol. Holding the weapon in both hands, she took a deep breath, then kicked open the door all the way, dropping into a firing crouch.

Dim light from the street and the alleyway spilled into the small apartment through the open blinds, laying down pale stripes on the walls and floor. Squeak's place had been a mess the first time Kellan had met with the warez dood, but now it looked like a bomb had gone off. Everything was overturned. Chips, casings, spare parts and scraps of electronics were scattered all over the floor. The one set of shelves had even been pulled down, their contents spilled across the room.

Kellan cautiously stepped further into the room, swinging her weapon right and then left to cover either side of the door. There was no one there.

"Squeak?" she called out softly. There was no answer. She moved deeper into the apartment, her nerves alert for the slightest sound, the slightest movement. She swung around the doorway into the small kitchen. It was dark and silent, dirty dishes piled up in the small sink, discarded food containers on the countertop. Then she noticed a faint light spilling out into the hall from a half-closed door.

Kellan found Squeak in the small bathroom. He was lying in the tub, completely dry and fully clothed. She crouched down and pressed her fingers to his carotid artery, but she knew before she touched him that he was dead. His skin had a bluish tinge and was even more pale and waxy than normal. She carefully lifted one slack hand. It fell loosely back over the side of the tub.

He hasn't been dead long, Kellan thought, since rigor mortis hadn't set in yet. She wished she knew exactly *how* long. Probably only a few hours. How long *did* it take for a corpse to stiffen up? Everything Kellan knew about forensics she learned from the trid and from hearing other shadowrunners talk. She looked closely at the warez dood's body. There was no blood, no sign of injury that she could see, no bruises on his neck or any other indication he was strangled.

"Aw, Squeak . . . " she muttered. *What the frag happened?*

Her first thought was a robbery. Some chipped-out punk, maybe even a group of them, busting down the door to rip off whatever they could sell. The place was certainly torn up enough, but it didn't explain the condition of the body. Gangers would have beaten Squeak to death or simply shot him, but there were no wounds, and no blood anywhere.

Suicide? Didn't seem likely. Squeak *might* have gone off the deep end if he figured out on his own that his weapons data was worthless, but why trash the place first? Anyway, he just didn't strike Kellan as the suicidal type.

She crouched beside the tub, looking at the still, slack-jawed face.

Magic? Now *that* was a definite possibility, and unfortunately there was only one way to be sure. Kellan focused her attention on the corpse and willed her perceptions to shift, opening herself to the impressions of the astral plane. She braced herself for whatever she might sense there. She knew it was going be like jumping into icy water.

It was cold, the recent impression of death. She was right; Squeak had died not long ago. Though his living aura was gone, traces of what he once was still clung to the body, like fragrance to a dead flower. But there was nothing else. Kellan saw no sign of any spell or spirit, no thread connected to a ritual—whatever caused Squeak's death, it wasn't magic.

Poison, Kellan thought, looking at the blue-tinged face and lips again. She wasn't sure what made that word leap into her mind. Was it something she sensed mystically about the body, or just intuition? Sometimes it was hard to tell the difference. Poison certainly fit with the condition of the body, particularly the lack of evidence of any kind of violence. A poison could have been administered in any number of ways that would leave no trace, and the body dumped into the tub after it had done its work.

Maybe drugs. . . . Kellan pondered that for a moment, but it didn't make sense either. Squeak was too much of a deckhead to bother with chemical mindbenders when there were so many digital choices available—simsense chips that could duplicate the effects of any drug you could imagine and more, all without the biochemical effects. Of course, he could have been chipping, but there was nothing in Squeak's datajack.

A noise caught Kellan's attention, and she allowed her astral perception to fade, shifting back to her mundane senses and standing up from her crouch beside the tub. She gripped the Crusader in both hands again and stepped quietly toward the door. Almost immediately, she heard someone, maybe more than one person, moving around in the main room of the apartment.

Kellan's heart raced, and she tightened her grip on the pistol. Maybe they were chummers of Squeak's; maybe they were just urban scavengers who saw an open door and an opportunity. She didn't know if they were armed, or how many were out there. So she stayed by the door of the bathroom, flattened against the wall, listening carefully to the sound of footsteps in the apartment beyond.

A hand opened the half-closed door and Kellan swung around, pistol leveled directly at the intruder.

"Holy drek!" he shouted.

"One move and you're dead," Kellan said as evenly as she could, and the guy immediately understood he was in no position to argue.

He was human and a Brain Eater, the latter made obvious by the red fez with a gold tassel tipped at a slight angle on his head—part of the gang's colors. He couldn't have been much more than sixteen or so. He was wearing loose-fitting cargo pants and a vest with numerous bulging pockets over a long-sleeved jersey. He was holding a palm-sized taser.

Kellan nodded toward it, and he dropped it on the floor with a clatter.

The Brain Eater's eyes flicked past Kellan to Squeak's body sprawled out in the tub.

"He's dead," Kellan said flatly.

"Then so are you," the ganger replied, mustering the courage to face her down. "You won't make it out of here."

"I didn't kill him."

"Yeah, right," he snorted.

"It's the truth," Kellan said, "I found him like this. We were working on some biz—"

"Keefer, what the frag're you doin' back there?" asked a voice from the direction of the kitchen. Then, "Holy drek!"

Kellan grabbed Keefer's arm and jerked him into the bathroom as another ganger appeared in the hallway, similar in age and dress. She locked her arm around the slender ganger's neck, pulling him back against her and pressing the muzzle of the Crusader into his side. His buddy's eyes widened in shock and he reflexively reached for his weapon.

"Don't," Kellan warned.

"Don't do it, Zoog!" Keefer gabbled in a panic, his meager bravado disappearing the instant he felt Kellan's Crusader against his body

"Who the frag are you?" the other ganger demanded.

"She killed Squeak!" Keefer blurted.

"I don't fraggin' have time for this," Kellan sighed. "I told your chummer here that Squeak and I had biz. I came in and found him dead."

"You expect us to believe that?" Zoog asked incredulously.

"I really don't fraggin' care what you believe," Kellan snapped. "I'm not lookin' for trouble. I'm going to walk out of here now, and your chummer is coming with me by way of insurance. He's the first one to catch it if the drek starts to fly. So let's all just stay nice and calm, and then nobody gets hurt, *wakarimasuka?*"

Zoog didn't seem to know what to do. All Kellan wanted was to clear out of Brain Eater turf before the situation got out of control. There didn't seem to be much chance of convincing the gangers she had nothing to do with Squeak's death, especially not while she was holding one of them hostage, but she didn't want to let Keefer go and lose her bargaining position. Right now, the best she could hope for was to get out of the warez dood's apartment in one piece. There would be time to smooth things over with the Brain Eaters later, if need be.

"How many more of you are there in the building?" Kellan asked. Zoog refused to answer, but Keefer stammered a response. "J-Just two more downstairs!"

Zoog glared at Keefer, but didn't contradict him— not with Kellan's gun still pressed against Keefer's ribs.

"All right," she said, still looking at Zoog. "Here's

how this is going to work. You're going to walk ahead of us, close enough that I can see you. We're going to go downstairs, and I'm going to leave. If you cause me grief, then Keefer here gets it"—she jammed the gun harder against his side—"and you're next."

"C'mon," Keefer begged, "just let me go. It's frosty! I swear we won't do anything! We didn't see a thing!"

Kellan shook her head. "Sorry, chummer. I can't afford to leave you two behind me, and I need to clear out of here." She gestured to Zoog with her Crusader. "Now move!"

The whole trip down the stairs, Kellan wished she had some of G-Dogg's size and strength. The ork bouncer could have juggled both Keefer and Zoog and barely worked up a sweat. Keefer was small for his age, but that still made him nearly the same size as Kellan. Sure, she had the drop on him, and she had the gun, but she really didn't want to use it. Bad enough the Brain Eaters thought she'd offed Squeak. If she blew away one of them, things would only get worse.

Fortunately, Keefer and Zoog didn't seem inclined to cause Kellan any grief. Zoog led the way down the stairs, with Kellan and Keefer following close behind. She kept an eye out for anyone else likely to cause trouble, but no one even bothered to poke their head out from behind the closed doors.

Two more Brain Eaters were kicking around in the

lobby, just like Keefer said. One was an ork, not as big as G-Dogg, but still a good half meter taller than Kellan. He wore a sleeveless shirt and vest, showing off arms rippling with muscle. The other ganger was older than the rest, maybe in his twenties. His hair was buzzed down to a fine dark stubble under his fez, and chrome rings pierced his eyebrow, lips and ears. Both gangers abruptly straightened away from the wall where they'd been leaning when they realized Kellan was holding Keefer at gunpoint.

"Chill!" Zoog said, patting the air with his palms. "It's frosty." The other two managed to keep still.

"What the frag is this?" the human asked, nodding toward Kellan and Keefer.

"This," Kellan replied, before anyone else could, "is a simple deal. I walk out of here, and Keefer doesn't get a lead implant tonight."

"She totally means it, Crash!" Keefer babbled. "She's fraggin' crazy!"

"Shut up," the bald ganger barked. His eyes narrowed, and he stared at Kellan for a moment.

"What's your name?" he asked.

"What does it matter?"

He shrugged. "It doesn't. You're dead either way."

"Well, unless you're going to make good on that threat, I suggest you get the frag out of my way."

"You *really* think you can take us all?" Crash growled.

"I don't need to take all of you," Kellan said, doing her best to keep her voice stone cold. "You just need to decide which of you wants to be the first to get plugged after Keefer here buys it." She jammed the Crusader into the ganger's side again for emphasis, and Keefer winced in her grip.

There was a long pause as Crash regarded Kellan across the narrow width of the lobby. Keefer made a faint whimpering sound. Kellan wondered if the ganger would be crazy enough to call her on her threat, or just sacrifice Keefer to get at her. That would be a first—and possibly a last—in her experience. She was counting on the fact that gangs took care of their own, no matter what.

Crash waved off Zoog and the ork, and took a step back, clearing the way to the door.

"This isn't over," he said.

"It is for now," Kellan replied.

"We'll find you," the ork growled. "You're dead."

"Whatever."

Kellan kept her hostage between her and the other Brain Eaters all the way to the door. She pushed the door open with her hip, stepping out onto the stairs. Then she simultaneously loosened her grip on Keefer's neck, planted her other hand in his back and shoved him into the lobby, stepping back to allow the door to swing shut.

Crash and the other Brian Eaters grabbed for their weapons, but Keefer was still in the way and Kellan had the drop on them. She raised her Crusader, pointing the muzzle up toward the ceiling. In her left hand, she created a faintly glowing sphere of light.

She hurled it at the gangers, barely whispering the word of power. The globe passed through the glass like sunlight and burst in a soundless flash. The Brain Eaters grabbed their heads, dropped their weapons and crumpled to the floor. The door clicked shut and locked.

Kellan looked at the helpless gangers for a moment. She could easily finish them off. A couple bursts from her Crusader, or a lethal spell . . . then no one would know what happened. No witnesses would be left to place her at the scene. But for what it was worth at this moment, she wasn't a cold-blooded killer. Other shadowrunners might consider it efficient to eliminate all traces of their presence, but Kellan wasn't one of them.

She left the Brain Eaters where they lay. Let them wonder why the person they thought killed Squeak bothered to leave them alive. Kellan holstered her pistol and mounted her motorcycle in the alley.

A faint buzz made Kellan jump, turn back toward the door and reach for her gun. Then she realized the vibration was coming from her phone. She fished it out of her pocket and looked at the display. She was receiving an e-mail. The originating address was unfamiliar, but the content of the message immediately caught Kellan's attention.

Kellan,
    If you're reading this, then something happened to me. (Frag, I always wanted to say that!)

Seriously, I've got a weird feeling about this deal. So I've set up a fail-safe to send you all my files in case something does happen. Once you read this message, the program frame will forward the files to your e-mail address. You'll know what to do with them.

I hope you make the score. I really liked you, Kellan, and I know you can make it. You're a kick-ass shadowrunner.

Squeak

Kellan felt a chill as she read the message and glanced up at the window of the apartment where Squeak lay dead. The warez dood's feelings were right on the money. She looked back at the phone's display. What if this was more than just another random act of Barrens violence? What if someone else knew about Squeak's data and, unlike Jackie, believed it would lead to a big payoff? They might have killed Squeak in order to get his files—or to make sure he didn't give them to anyone else.

Did they find the data? The place certainly was torn up, but a tech-head like Squeak wouldn't leave paydata just lying around. He would have stored it somewhere safe, in some online hidey-hole that no one else could find.

She watched the icon flash on the phone's display screen for a moment before thumbing the READ key to download the files. The phone buzzed to indicate they were stored in its removable memory. Then Kellan snapped the phone closed and put it back in her jacket pocket. She suddenly felt sure of it: somebody thought Squeak's data was valuable enough that they needed to kill him to keep it quiet.

Squeak thought Kellan had what it took to follow the mystery through to the end. She thought, *This isn't over. I am going to see it through.* She kicked over the Rapier's engine. There was work to do.

8

Kellan had never recruited shadowrunners entirely on her own. Back in Kansas City, the shadow community was small enough that you knew everyone worth knowing, and word of potential work spread quickly. Informal teams assembled as needed, and many of them became pretty tight-knit. When she was learning the ropes of the shadow biz, Kellan was never involved in putting teams together—she just wanted to make sure they included her. Since her arrival in Seattle, Kellan got her jobs from movers and shakers like G-Dogg and Lothan. The one time she'd put together a team, she'd gotten her contacts from G-Dogg, whose mind was an inexhaustible database of names and places. Kellan was counting on that knowledge now.

G-Dogg answered his phone on the second ring. "Talk to me," he said.

"Hey, G-Dogg."

"Hey, Kellan, 'sup?"

"I need a little help."

"Sure thing. What do you need?" G-Dogg asked.

"Some names," Kellan replied. There was a long pause on the other end of the line.

"You're not still looking to put together that run you told us about, are you?" G-Dogg asked.

Kellan had expected this reaction. "Look, G-Dogg, if you don't want to help—"

"Hey, chill!" the ork protested. "I didn't say that. I just want to know if you're still set on doing this run, that's all."

"I'm doing it," Kellan said firmly, "and I need some talent."

G-Dogg sighed. "There's no way I can talk you out of this?"

"No. Look, G-Dogg, I need to do this, okay? I'd like your help. I'm not asking you to buy into the run. I just need some names."

The ork sighed again. "Most runners I'm willing to work with aren't going to be interested in a run like this," he began.

"But I bet you know some that might be," Kellan concluded.

"Yeah, a couple."

"Put me in touch with them. After that, you're out of it, G-Dogg, I swear." When the ork hesitated, she went on. "If you can't help me, that's cool. I'll post the job on Shadowland, and ask around a few other places."

"Okay, okay, I want to help," G-Dogg said. "I know a few runners who will take on high-risk jobs, especially if the run has the potential for a big payoff."

"This run has got a lot of potential."

"*And* a lot of risk. But hey, that's for them to decide. I'm sending you the contact info now." A moment later Kellan's phone beeped to indicate G-Dogg's incoming download. She stored the virtual business cards in the phone's memory.

"Just remember, Kellan," the ork bouncer warned her. "These guys aren't like the runners you've worked with before. They're willing to take risks either because they're desperate or because they *like* it, for one reason or another. Runners worth working with don't take unnecessary risks." He left the remainder of the criticism unspoken, but the message was clear: which category did Kellan want to fit into?

"Thanks," she said dryly. "I promise I'll be careful. I owe you one, G."

"Yeah," he said. "Buy me a drink and tell me all about it when it's over, and we'll consider it even, okay?" He paused. "Good luck, kid," he said, then he hung up.

Kellan looked at the information she'd downloaded to her phone. G-Dogg had given her a depressingly short list, but on the bright side, it wouldn't take her long to make the calls. Plus, she had a few resources of her own she could tap. She highlighted the first name on the list and hit CALL.

It didn't take Kellan long to work her way through G-Dogg's list. Within ten minutes she'd set up a couple of meets, been turned down by a couple of potentials, and left messages for the rest.

Still buzzing on the adrenaline from her adventure in the Barrens, Kellan knew she'd go stir-crazy if she just sat around and waited for the phone to ring, so she grabbed her jacket and headed out. Like most shadowrunners, she'd adopted a largely nocturnal lifestyle, sleeping late and staying up later. Business was best done in the dark, and nighttime was when Seattle's shadows really came to life.

Business at Underworld 93 was starting to heat up when she arrived. The club was housed in a renovated industrial warehouse, a massive two-story block of ferrocrete with windows covered in heavy metal mesh. Neolux letters a meter high spelled out its name across the marquee, and as usual, a line of hopeful club-goers stretched out the door and around the block. Kellan pulled her bike into the alley, parking it alongside the others already there.

The Underworld was the first nightspot Kellan had visited when she arrived in Seattle. She smiled to herself when she thought about how different things were then. Then she had been a complete newbie, taking a Grid-Cab to the club and bluffing her way past the bouncer looking for G-Dogg, whom she'd heard was a potential contact. Little had she known the bouncer at the door *was* G-Dogg, and that he didn't know her from a hole in the wall. If it hadn't been for an unwanted altercation with some troll gangers, the Spikes, Kellan might never have gotten G-Dogg's attention—or discovered her magical abilities, for that matter. She'd cast her first spell that night, turning one of the trolls into a metahuman torch. It earned her an introduction to Lothan and to the Seattle shadows.

After that, Underworld 93 became a familiar haunt for Kellan, since it was fairly close to where she lived in Puyallup and one of the hottest nightspots in the metroplex. G-Dogg worked there on a regular basis, but Kellan knew tonight the ork bouncer was elsewhere, which suited her just fine. She really wasn't in the mood to face any of her current shadowrunning associates.

With a smile and a subtle donation of nuyen to the bouncer working the door, Kellan slipped past the line to enter the Underworld. As always, the club had a live act on stage and people crowded on the dance floor. Kellan wended her way through the crush to reach the bar running along the back wall.

"Hey, Leif," she greeted the elven bartender. He was tall and blond, and he flashed Kellan a smile as she approached.

"Hey, Kellan, zappinin'?"

"Same ol'," she replied and the elf nodded sagely.

"Usual?" he asked, and Kellan nodded. The elf popped the top on a bottle of beer and slid it across the counter to her. Kellan slotted her credstick into the bar's payport and it automatically deducted the price of the drink. She added a tip before removing her credstick and pocketing it again. Then she rocked back on one of the barstools, sipped her drink, watched the crowd and listened to the band get ready for their show.

They played a good set. Their style of Celtic fusion metal wasn't usually to Kellan's taste, but the lead singer boasted great vocals and the compelling stage presence typical of an elf. Their synth player was also excellent. He was plugged directly into the instrument, and played it using the neural interface. He achieved much finer control of the instrument than any player could achieve with his hands, and his skill boosted the band's performance way above the ordinary.

The band was breaking down after their set, and Kellan was still at the bar nursing her second beer when a beautiful woman emerged from the crowd and leaned into the bar near her. She was an elf, with the striking features of her race: high cheekbones, almond-shaped eyes and delicately pointed ears. Her skin was fair, pale in contrast to her raven-black hair, which was pulled tightly into a ponytail at the nape of her neck, highlighting her ears and graceful, up-swept brows. She wore black leather pants that fit her like a glove, a silvery button-down shirt under a short leather jacket, and slim black boots with pointed toes.

She spoke briefly with Leif, who poured her a

drink. After she paid for it, she turned to look at Kellan, then moved down the bar toward her.

"Hello. . . . Kellan, isn't it?" she asked.

Kellan was surprised the woman knew her name, but she saw no reason to deny it. She nodded.

"I'm called Midnight," the elf said. "I've actually been hoping to meet you," she continued. "I've heard good things about you. And I heard through contacts earlier tonight that you're putting together a run." She paused, and looked at Kellan more closely, a curious expression on her face. "More importantly, though, I think I may have known your mother."

"What?" Kellan asked, her cool, professional demeanor momentarily forgotten. "How? When?"

"Let's talk, shall we?" Midnight invited. She gestured toward the tables off to the side of the dance floor, allowing Kellan to lead the way. She seemed completely unaware of the admiring looks her catlike grace drew on the way.

As they slid into chairs on opposite sides of the table, Midnight studied Kellan closely, sitting back comfortably in her chair and crossing one shapely leg over the other.

"So, you knew my mother?" Kellan asked, barely managing to control her curiosity.

"Well, I'm not certain, of course," Midnight said. "It's just that I knew a woman who looked quite a bit like you, and you seem the right age to be her daughter, if she had one. She was my mentor when

I first started working in the shadows, and she wore a necklace just like yours."

Kellan's hand went to the amulet she wore on a chain around her neck. It was made of green jade, carved in a simple yet intricately detailed design of a dragon coiled into a circle. It had arrived at her aunt's house in Kansas City in a package along with a few other items and a note that said, *This stuff belonged to your mother. Thought you might want it.* The package had no return address, but it did have a Seattle postmark. She didn't remember her mother at all, and she had come to the metroplex hoping to track down the sender, and maybe find out what became of her mother.

"You're sure?" she asked, and Midnight nodded.

"Absolutely," she said. "That amulet is quite unique. The woman I knew had one just like it, and I doubt there are two of them."

Kellan could hardly believe her luck. After months of searching and finding nothing, someone who knew her mother had turned up looking for work!

"It *was* my mother's," she told Midnight. "I mean . . . I was told it was my mother's. I never knew her."

"Oh. Well, truthfully, I didn't know she had a kid, assuming it's the same woman."

"Tell me about her." Kellan suddenly realized how intense she sounded. "Um, that is, if you wouldn't mind."

"Of course not." Midnight gave her a dazzling

smile. She took a sip of her drink, set it back down on the table, then folded her hands beside it.

"It's been nearly twenty years since I came to Seattle from Tir Tairngire." She pronounced the name of the elven nation south of Seattle with an exotic lilt in her voice. "I think I was probably about your age. I wanted to work in the shadows, but I didn't know a thing about life in the metroplex or the shadows. I had the great good fortune of hooking up almost immediately with a woman called Mustang. She was a shadowrunner with a good reputation who was willing to work with a newbie and show her the ropes.

"She taught me so much. We worked together for a couple of years, and I learned how to run the shadows like a pro. Then, one day, she disappeared."

"So you don't know what happened to her?"

Midnight shook her head. "I never found out. I actually was hoping you might know. I didn't even know Mustang had a daughter, though you must have been born after I met her."

"How did you find out about me?" Kellan asked.

Midnight smiled. "I still do a lot of work in the shadows," she said. "Particularly finding things people want to have, or want to know about. Simon Brickman wanted to know about you."

"Brickman. . . ." Kellan recognized the name of the company man working for Knight Errant Security Services who had hired Lothan's team for Kellan's first shadowrun in Seattle. It turned out Brickman planned the run simply as cover for a scheme to funnel weapons made by Knight Errant's parent company, Ares Macrotechnology, to Seattle gangs. Kellan had put a kink in that plan. She gave Midnight a wary look.

"Don't worry!" she told Kellan. "I told him there wasn't anything to find, really, that you were just a kid who got lucky. I recognized your amulet, you see, and I wanted to talk to you in person."

"Why didn't you get in touch before this?"

"Business," Midnight said simply. "Other work came along after I finished the job for Brickman, and I didn't have a chance to follow up. Also, I tried to find out more about what happened to Mustang before I got in touch with you, so that I'd have something more concrete to tell you, but I'm sorry to say I wasn't able to turn up anything else."

Kellan opened her mouth to respond, then closed it again. She wasn't sure what she felt. She realized that it had been so many months since she'd followed any solid leads on her mother or the origin of the mysterious package she'd received that there was a part of her that had started to give up hope. Now when she finally met someone who actually might have known her mother, that hope had been instantly renewed—then crushed again when it became clear that Midnight didn't know anything more about her mother's fate than did Kellan.

"How frustrating for you," Midnight said, echoing her thoughts. "I wish there was more I could tell you."

"It's okay," Kellan replied, shaking her head. "I found out more tonight than I've managed to discover the whole time I've been in Seattle. . . . So, you say I look like her?"

"Oh, there's a definite resemblance," Midnight replied with a smile. "You've got her hair, her eyes, her chin."

"What was she like?"

The elven woman thought for a moment, searching for the right words. "Forceful," she said. "Dynamic, smart, talented and savvy. She was good—one of the best."

"Talented. . . ." Kellan repeated. "Was she a magician?"

Midnight frowned slightly and shook her head. "Not that I know of, why?"

"Oh," was all Kellan said. She had assumed that since her mother's amulet was magical, and Kellan had the Talent, her mother must have been a magician, too. Midnight's reaction to that suggestion meant her mother must have been mundane. Or maybe her mother's talent had been latent and had never awakened. Or maybe her Talent came from her father. . . .

Kellan noticed that Midnight was looking at something behind her just as a looming shadow fell across the table.

"Lothan," Kellan said, looking up at the troll mage. He stood within arm's reach of the table. Kellan kicked herself for sitting with her back to the crowd.

Midnight had maneuvered to take the seat against the wall of the club without her noticing. Otherwise, she would have seen Lothan approach. Now she felt at a disadvantage.

"Kellan. Interesting company you're keeping these days."

"Lothan, always a pleasure to see you, too," Midnight said, though her smile said all of the pleasure came from the fact that her presence annoyed Lothan.

Does Lothan know everyone? Kellan wondered, watching the exchange. Of course, the old troll had been in the shadow biz longer than anyone else Kellan knew—longer, in fact, than most of the other shadowrunners she knew had been alive. Still, it was an interesting coincidence, Lothan showing up here and now. If it was a coincidence.

"I'd introduce you," Kellan said to Lothan, "but it seems like you already—"

"Know each other?" Midnight interjected. "Oh, yes. Everyone knows Lothan, of course. His reputation precedes him."

"The same might be said of you," Lothan told Midnight.

"I prefer to keep a lower profile," the elf said. "Not that it's difficult, by comparison."

"No doubt. Kellan, might I have a word with you?" Lothan asked.

Just at that moment, Kellan felt the vibration of her phone ringing.

"Hang on," she said, pulling it from the pocket of her jacket. "Hello?"

"Kellan, what's this I hear about you following up on the run?" Jackie Ozone's voice sounded concerned. *Frag, word gets around fast.* Kellan wondered if G-Dogg had said something to Jackie. On the other hand, finding things out was what Jackie did best.

"I can't really talk right now," Kellan said in a neutral tone, glancing at Midnight and Lothan. The elf got to her feet, slipping a slim hand over Lothan's massive arm and giving a winning smile.

"Let's give Kellan some privacy, shall we? We can catch up on old times," she said, just loud enough for Kellan to hear, then guided Lothan away from the table.

"What kind of game do you think you're playing at, Midnight?" Lothan demanded as soon as they were a few steps away from the table and out of earshot.

"I could ask you the same thing, Lothan," she replied, raising her dark eyebrows in a question. "Imagine my surprise, after making arrangements with you to buy information about certain trinkets that might cross your path, to stumble across the amulet hanging around that girl's neck."

"What do you want with it?"

"As I told you when we made our deal, that's my business."

"Well, I'm making it *my* business, Midnight."

"Lothan, Lothan," she purred, running her fingers along his arm. "You're not a fool. Don't act like one. Do you *really* want to cross me over this?"

"I'm warning you, Midnight, stay away from Kellan."

"Or what?" the elf asked. "You'll tell her the truth? I'm surprised you still know it when you see it. I've done my homework, Lothan. Kellan has been working with you too long to still consider you a paragon of virtue. Besides, what will you tell her? That I commissioned you to keep an eye out for a certain item, and when it came along, you 'forgot' to inform me? Maybe so you could keep the information—and the amulet—to yourself?"

Midnight paused, and Lothan's face darkened. "Yes," she hissed, "that's what I thought. The only truth you'll end up revealing, my dear Lothan, is that you've lied to your young apprentice yet again. Then you can forget about what little trust she still has left in you. I, on the other hand, have nothing to fear from your story. After all, Kellan already knows I was interested in her amulet. I just told her so. I haven't mentioned *your* involvement in this, however, and I won't . . . unless you force my hand.

"So the next move is really up to you, isn't it?" she asked sweetly.

"Okay," Kellan said, once Lothan and Midnight had moved away from the table.

"So you're going to follow up on Squeak's data," Jackie stated, in a tone that made it clear she didn't approve. "It's a waste of time and money, Kellan. Like I told you, that data isn't worth the chip it's burned on."

"Look, I trust your advice, Jackie—really, I do. But I've got a feeling about this that I can't ignore," Kellan said. "I don't think the data is worthless."

"Look, Kellan, I'm sure your chummer Squeak thinks he's struck gold, but—"

"Squeak's dead."

There was a moment of silence on the other end of the line.

"What?" Jackie said.

"Squeak's dead," Kellan repeated.

"Are you sure?"

"Oh yeah, I'm sure. I found him earlier tonight, in his apartment, in the bathtub. I think he was poisoned. There wasn't a mark on him, and no signs of magic that I could assense."

"And you think someone killed him because of this data?"

"It would be a huge coincidence otherwise," Kellan said.

"That makes going after it even more stupid, Kellan!" Jackie exclaimed. "If someone is willing to kill for this . . ."

"Then it must be worth something," Kellan concluded. "It must be worth a *lot*."

"You don't know that," the decker countered. "He

might have been killed over something else entirely. Even if you're right—well, people getting killed means you're in over your head, Kellan. It's better to just let it go."

"I can't. Not now. When I started this, it was just my shot at putting together a run of my own. Now, it's something I owe to Squeak. He believed in me."

"And look where it got him," Jackie shot back, and Kellan winced. "I'm sorry, Kellan, I didn't mean it the way it sounded. But Squeak's dead. Going on this run isn't going to make any difference to him."

"It'll make a difference to *me*," Kellan said. Then, "I assume I can rely on your professional discretion regarding this."

"Of course. But you have to understand, I'm out—if you want to do this, you're on your own."

"Understood," Kellan replied coolly. "You've done enough already."

"Kellan, listen to me," Jackie's tone almost sounded pleading. "Let it go. This one is trouble. Trust me."

"I'm going to see it through, Jackie. I'll let you know how it turns out." She hung up and slipped the phone back into her pocket, glancing over to where Lothan and Midnight were talking. Lothan caught her eye for a moment, like he wanted to come over and say something, then he turned and walked away, slipping through the crowd on the dance floor. Midnight came back to the table and sat back down opposite Kellan.

"What was that all about?" Kellan asked.

"Lothan had to go," Midnight said.

"No, I mean what is it with you and Lothan?"

"Lothan and I have . . . history," Midnight said lightly. "We don't always see eye to eye on things."

Kellan snorted. "Tell me about it. Lothan seems to have that effect on people."

"Ah, you've noticed," Midnight said with a smile. "Let's just say I've noticed Lothan is a great mage . . ."

". . . but not always the most diplomatic?" the elf concluded.

"Exactly," Kellan said.

"Well, he doesn't seem to think you should be keeping company with the likes of me."

"Lothan's not the boss of me," Kellan said stubbornly. "I just take magic lessons from him. I can 'keep company' with whomever I want."

Midnight raised an eyebrow slightly. "You *are* Lothan's student, then," she said.

Kellan dismissed it as nothing with a wave of her hand. "Yeah, he's teaching me magic."

"Is that why you asked if your mother had the Talent?"

Kellan blushed slightly. "I figured she might, since I do."

"Well, there's always your father . . . " Midnight offered, again echoing Kellan's own thoughts. "Do you know anything about him?"

"Even less than I know about my mother," Kellan

113

said with a sigh. "My aunt—my mom's older sister—raised me, and she said she never even met my father, and that my mom never talked about him. I was hoping you knew something."

"Well, if I can help you find out anything more, I will," Midnight said, putting her hand on Kellan's arm.

"Thanks," she said.

"I owe Mustang a lot. If it weren't for her, I wouldn't be where I am today."

There was a pause. Kellan didn't know quite what to say. Midnight was the only connection she'd found to her mother in all her time in Seattle. The elf was also one of the only people in the shadows who'd offered to help, who obviously felt the same sense of duty Kellan felt to the people in her life.

"So . . . " Midnight broke the silence. "It sounds like you have some biz in the works. Unless that call means things didn't work out . . . ?"

"No, that was something else," Kellan said. "I've got a run lined up—actually, it's more of an opportunity. . . ."

"I'd be interested in hearing about it, if you'd like to tell me. Maybe I can help."

"Well, I don't kn—" Kellan began.

"It's up to you," Midnight interrupted, "but I have experience and contacts, and I'd like to help out if I can. It would be like paying back your mother for the help she gave me."

That was all it took. Kellan gave Midnight the

cover story she'd developed about finding data that indicated the existence of an old United States weapons cache or military installation somewhere in Salish-Shidhe territory. She was professionally vague about the details, including Squeak's involvement.

"The problem," Kellan concluded, "is that even if I find the location I need, there might be nothing there. If there *is* something there . . ."

"Then you need a buyer," Midnight concluded. "Sounds to me like you could also use a patron who's willing to fund some of this expedition. In my experience, shadowrunners are more willing to deal with unknowns when there's money up front."

Kellan shrugged. "But I don't know anyone like that."

Midnight smiled conspiratorially. "Yes, you do. It's just a matter of asking in the right way."

Kellan listened as the elf explained her plan, and a slow smile crept across her face.

9

"Explain to me again why I agreed this was a good idea," Kellan commented as the two women waited in the dark for the arrival of their contact.

"Because it *is* a good idea," Midnight countered, "if I do say so myself."

"Do you really think he'll show?"

"Oh, he'll be here," the elf said. "He's nothing if not punctual."

"I hope so. Cuz this isn't a great place to wait around," Kellan replied.

It was called Squatter's Mall, and it was the largest quasi-legal market in the Redmond Barrens. When the economy of the Redmond area went south in the Crash, retailers pulled out of the depressed area in herds, leaving entire shopping centers and malls abandoned. That sent Redmond even deeper into its economic death spiral, and it never recovered. Now the district was full of empty malls, office parks and other real estate no one in their right mind would touch. Of course, most of the inhabitants of Redmond weren't exactly in their right minds.

Squatters set up housekeeping in the abandoned shops, and many opened for business, selling their wares from blankets on the sidewalks or displaying them on the store shelves. The mall functioned as a sprawling flea market during the day. At night, most of the businesses shut down, and the squatters retreated behind crude barricades. The corridors of the mall were open territory for anyone to pass—at least in theory.

"Why'd he suggest meeting here?" Kellan asked, glancing around as casually as she could for any sign of trouble. The few people in the mall at this late hour gave them no more than sidelong glances and kept moving. "Since we're both on the south side . . ."

Midnight shrugged. "Who knows? Maybe he likes the ambience. He obviously wanted to handle it outside the office, particularly since we don't exactly keep regular hours."

"I just wish he'd get here," Kellan muttered.

"Then you've got your wish," Midnight said. "Over there."

She followed Midnight's glance, and a moment later she spotted him. Her eyes didn't adjust to the gloom inside the old mall quite as well as an elf's, but now she could clearly make out the figure walking toward them.

"Remember," Midnight said in a low voice, "odds are good he's not alone, even if you can't see anyone with him." Kellan nodded in acknowledgment of the warning.

He was just as she recalled: medium height, well built, and dressed in a casual outfit that probably cost enough to feed half the squatters in the mall. He wore all black, from his button-down shirt and tailored slacks to his zipped-up synthleather coat and polished shoes. His dark hair was neatly trimmed, and wraparound shades concealed his eyes. He wore wrist-length black leather gloves, but kept his hands clearly visible outside the pockets of his jacket as he approached them.

"Midnight," he said with a curt nod toward the elf, "and Kellan Colt, about whom I have heard so much." His smile contained no warmth as he extended his hand. Kellan took it. His handshake was firm and solid.

"Mr. Brickman," she replied.

"Oh, so formal," he said. "You can call me Simon, if you like. I feel like we've gotten to know each other a little better after our first meeting."

"You've gotten to know *me* better, you mean."

Brickman smiled. "Well, I'm practically an open book."

"*The Art of War*, if I remember correctly," Midnight interjected. "Or was it *How to Climb the Corporate Ladder*, Simon?"

"Both favorites of mine," he replied mildly. "But I don't think you asked me here to start a book club."

"No, we have business," Kellan said.

"So Midnight said. Well, I'm here, and I'm quite interested in hearing your proposal. Don't worry," he said, gesturing with one gloved hand. "Our conversation will remain private. My people will see to that."

Kellan noted the confirmation of Midnight's warning that Brickman wouldn't be alone. He was making it equally clear he had nothing to fear from them, if this meeting was some sort of trap. She glanced at Midnight, who nodded, indicating Kellan should proceed as they discussed on the way to the meeting.

So Kellan outlined the deal for Brickman. She told him about the possible take, and what she thought was involved in getting it. She provided just enough detail to tantalize, without revealing the source of her information or the exact whereabouts of the target.

"Interesting," Brickman said when she was finished, "but is it really worthwhile?"

"You don't think so?" Kellan asked.

The company man gave an expressive shrug. "We are talking about materiel that's years, decades, out of date," he said, "and it's not like Ares is lacking in that area."

"But this materiel can't be traced back to you," Kellan replied. "These are goods nobody else knows about, and that won't require making resources from your own company disappear in order to use them."

"That *has* caused a few complications." Brickman's voice suddenly held a touch of steel, and Kellan wondered if she'd pressed him too far. After all, she was the cause of those "complications." If Brickman was carrying a grudge . . .

"Exclusive rights on whatever we find," Midnight offered.

"*If* you find anything," Brickman countered.

"We'll find something," Kellan said.

Brickman looked at her, his expression unreadable. "All right," he said. "I'm always interested in trying out new talent, and Midnight vouches for you. I'll put up some cred toward expenses in exchange for the exclusive rights to whatever you find, with the terms of that sale to be negotiated once the merchandise is on the table. However"—he raised a finger—"there are a few conditions."

"Name 'em," she said.

"First, I want Midnight in on this run. To be blunt, I know Midnight and her reputation, and I'll be more confident if I know an experienced runner is involved."

"No problem," Kellan said. "She's already in, if she wants to be."

Brickman smiled. "Good. Second"—he held up two fingers—"I expect a return on this investment. I want to see measurable progress within a week. If you don't have anything by then, you can consider our deal off."

Kellan nodded.

"Third," Brickman continued, "if it turns out there isn't anything worth salvaging, then you're owed nothing further. I'll cover the initial expenses, but your arrangements with your team are your own business, as are any further expenses you may incur. I'm not funding an expedition."

"Is that it?" Kellan asked. Brickman nodded.

"That's all," he said. He withdrew a credstick from an inner pocket of his jacket. "This contains your initial expenses in certified credit. Spend it wisely, because I'm not handing over any more until I see some results."

"Fine," she said, extending her hand. Brickman dropped the credstick into it.

"Good hunting, then," he said. He turned, with a nod toward Midnight, and walked away, leaving the two shadowrunners to begin planning how to earn the money he'd just handed them.

It was into the early hours of a new day by the time Kellan and Midnight made plans to get together later and went their separate ways. Kellan headed back to her apartment, looking forward to a few hours of sleep before she started putting together the team for her run.

Her run. It had a nice sound to it—one Kellan could get used to. She was feeling good about how she'd managed things so far. Though she didn't know for certain what Squeak's data would lead to, she was confident it was something important. Why else would someone have kacked Squeak, if not because of what he'd found out?

Kellan was also feeling good about the prospect of working with Midnight. She'd only known the other shadowrunner for a few hours, and already felt closer to her than to Lothan, G-Dogg or the other runners she'd worked with in Seattle. Midnight treated Kellan like an equal, not like some kid learning the ropes. She advised, but she clearly accepted that this was Kellan's run, and that she was calling the shots.

Plus there was the fact Midnight knew Kellan's mother, Mustang. Finally, Kellan had a lead! Though Midnight didn't know anything about her mother's current whereabouts, she was still a vital link to the past that she knew so little about. She felt sure that Midnight would have other clues that she could use to find her mother.

On the way home, Kellan wondered how she'd ever be able to sleep. She was buzzing with anticipation, eager to get started. Still, by the time she climbed off her motorcycle and trudged up the stairs to her doss, she was feeling the strain of the day's events. With a few hours of sleep, she'd be ready to tackle the next step.

She made sure the door was closed and locked before she dropped her bag and jacket on the floor next to it. She opened the fridge, grimacing at the brightness of the light and the barrenness of its interior. She settled for grabbing a bottle of water and drinking a few swigs before capping it and putting it back on the nearly empty shelf next to some Thai leftovers that were probably developing a civilization of their own.

"We really should talk about establishing some wards around this place," a voice said behind Kellan. She slammed the fridge door shut and spun around, drawing her Crusader from its shoulder holster in one smooth motion. The short barrel of the gun stuck right into the chest of the person behind her. Not really a person, but a ghostly image of one, through which Kellan's weapon passed harmlessly.

Lothan the Wise stood—hovered, rather—in the middle of Kellan's tiny kitchen. The troll mage was wearing his familiar robes, the mystic runes along the edges glimmering like gold. In one hand he held his gnarled wooden staff, the crystal on top of it giving off a soft light.

"*Fraggit*, Lothan!" Kellan said, lowering her gun. "Don't *do* that!"

"My apologies," the mage replied with a shrug. "Knocking is somewhat problematic in this state of being."

"How did you even know I was here?" Kellan asked, putting the Crusader back into its holster.

"I left a watcher to await your return," he said. "It informed me you were back."

"Now you're watching me behind my back?"

"Hardly," Lothan replied dryly. "I simply didn't want to waste time waiting, but I did want to talk to you."

There was a note in the old troll's voice that was unfamiliar to Kellan. Could it be that Lothan was actually worried about something?

"Okay, you're here," she said briskly. "So talk."

"Very well," Lothan said. He drew up his legs so he was sitting cross-legged, hovering about a half meter off the floor, his staff laid across his massive thighs. That put his horned head almost level with Kellan's face. Lothan closed his eyes for a moment, then looked directly at Kellan.

"Please keep in mind that I considered very carefully before coming to you about this. It's not my wont to interfere in the affairs of others."

Kellan snorted derisively, earning a glare from the old mage that silenced her. Lothan was only partially masking his aura; it flared with a tinge of anger, then faded back to the dull glow of concern. Kellan reminded herself that Lothan was an extremely powerful mage—something she would forget at her risk. She forced herself to speak politely.

"It's about Midnight, isn't it?" she asked. "What is it with you two?"

"As you know," Lothan responded, "Midnight and I share a history. Be wary of her, Kellan, for she isn't necessarily what she appears."

"Oh? Then what is she, Lothan? Tell me about the 'history' you share."

His face darkened in anger for a moment, then Lothan sighed heavily.

"It isn't important for you to know our history. I can only ask you to trust me on this. I know," he continued as Kellan opened her mouth to reply. "I know full well how it sounds. I know you don't entirely trust me, and you're right to reserve your suspicions. But consider; if you won't trust me, whom you know, why then do you trust Midnight?"

"Who says I do?" Kellan asked.

"Don't you? Kellan, I don't need special powers to guess where you've been tonight."

"You're not my father."

Lothan's face and aura darkened again. "No. No, I'm not. But I am supposed to be your teacher, Kellan, and I need to teach you the hard lessons, as well as the easier ones. One of the hardest lessons to accept is that you can't trust *anyone* in this business."

"Oh, you taught me that lesson, all right," Kellan shot back accusingly. "You taught me really well. But you know what? You say I shouldn't trust people, but G-Dogg helped me out when I needed him. Jackie, and Silver Max, and Liada haven't set me up to fail. Frag, even Orion trusted me enough to believe me when I told him the Ancients were being played by Brickman. Midnight hasn't given me any reason to mistrust her. In fact, the only person I've met in Seattle so far who has proved he can't be trusted is *you*, Lothan."

Lothan's face remained expressionless. When it

was clear that Kellan was finished, Lothan simply nodded. "You've made yourself clear. I'll see you for our next lesson, I hope. Good night, Kellan."

Then the troll mage's astral form faded from view. Kellan stood for a moment in her small kitchen, hugging her arms close to her chest. A faint chill seemed to linger in the air; Lothan could provide a very long-winded explanation for the effect, no doubt.

Kellan snorted. Lothan thought he knew all the answers. He was more than willing to give them to her, except when it came to the answers she *really* wanted. Like, why was he so interested in keeping her from associating with Midnight?

10

Simon Brickman stepped into his office, and paused when the lights didn't come on automatically, as they'd been programmed to do.

"Lights," he said, but the room remained dark.

"I think it's better if we have some shadows, don't you, Simon?" said a voice in the darkness. Then the lamp on his desk flicked to life, casting a small pool of illumination on the reflective surface. The light revealed the slim, dark-clad form of Midnight sitting in his chair, feet propped up on his desk.

Brickman closed the office door behind him.

"It's not as if either of us needs that much light," Midnight continued. She swung her long legs down off the desk and stood, then came around to lean against the edge of the desktop. "We're creatures of shadow, each in our own way."

"I'd ask how you got in here," Brickman said, stepping past Midnight and around the desk to his chair, "but I'm sure it will be in your regular security report. You do keep finding new ways around our system, don't you?"

"As long as there's a way, I'll find it," she said. She slid up to sit on the desk, leaning in on one hand so she could turn and face Brickman. He sank down into his chair, the snythleather still warm from Midnight's body. He put his hands behind his head, leaned back, and looked up at her.

"And what sort of game are you playing at now?" he asked.

"Game? Whatever do you mean?" the shadowrunner asked, fluttering her eyelashes at him.

Brickman smiled. "The girl, Kellan Colt, and this shadowrun of hers. You've already provided me with all the data there was to find on her, and I paid you for it. So why this interest in her, and why involve me in this run? I can only assume I'm throwing away good money on your say-so."

"Possibly not," Midnight said. "As I recall, Ares Macrotechnology inherited a lot of contracts from United States military suppliers after the Ghost Dance War. Some of those contracts included disarmament of old military depots, didn't they?"

"So? What if they did?" Brickman asked.

"It seems to me that finding an old military installation, perhaps one Ares might have—shall we say overlooked?—might be worthwhile. Especially if it contains materiel or information the UCAS, the CAS, the NAN, or any number of other parties might find interesting."

"It could also be an international incident if it's not handled right," Brickman observed. "You still haven't answered my question. Why the interest in this girl? You're not telling me you couldn't have gotten the information away from her if you really thought it was so valuable. Why are you letting her think she's calling the shots on this run?"

Midnight smiled impishly. "I have my reasons," she said. "Let's just say for the moment I see considerable potential in Kellan—qualities calling for a suitable mentor to help bring her to her full potential."

"You?"

"Why not?" Midnight asked. "Think of it as my way of giving back to the shadows after they have given so much to me."

Brickman's snort said what he thought of that idea. Still, he left it alone for the moment. It was clear Midnight wasn't going to give him a better explanation for her actions.

"Well," he said, "just be certain my nuyen isn't being misspent. I expect a complete report, Midnight, and I expect you to remember who you're really working for on this run."

"Oh, Simon," Midnight laughed. "You know I always look out for number one."

Lothan the Wise sighed deeply and opened his eyes. His usual meditation techniques were failing to calm his mind, and he was having trouble sleeping—not that he slept a great deal to begin with. He ponderously levered himself up out of the heavy, cushioned chair where he sat, ignoring the creaks and aches in his joints. He made his way from his study into his home's small kitchen, where he set the kettle to boil and poked in the cabinets for some tea.

Curse Midnight, anyway! The elf was devious—Lothan knew *that* better than most—and she was certainly up to something. It worried him that he didn't know exactly what. Oh, she wanted the amulet, of that he had no doubt. Lothan had been quite surprised when he'd seen it around Kellan's neck months ago. Midnight had contacted him about the amulet . . . it must have been nearly ten years ago. She gave Lothan a detailed description, never saying why she was interested in it, only that she would pay handsomely for information on its whereabouts. Lothan had all but forgotten about it until Kellan walked through the door of his study.

Having seen the amulet and examined it for himself, Lothan knew even less about why Midnight wanted it. The object was clearly enchanted, but it was like nothing else Lothan had ever seen. It seemed to act as a power focus for Kellan, but there was more to it than that. It seemed connected to her in some way Lothan couldn't fully explain. It was more than just the bond between a magician and her magical tools, it was . . . well, he didn't have a name for it, and that bothered him, too. In all his years of studying magic, Lothan had accumulated a vast amount of knowledge. To have such a mystery right in front of him was both tantalizing and frustrating.

The kettle began to whistle and Lothan absent-mindedly waved a hand at it from where he sat. The steaming kettle floated up off the burner and over to the teapot, where it tipped and began pouring boiling water onto the tea. Then Lothan waved it over to a cold burner, and shut the stove off with a flick of his fingers. He'd let the tea steep for a bit. The infusion of herbs might help to calm his nerves after his encounter with Kellan. He should have known he would find her so obstinate about the whole matter with Midnight. The elf had a charming way about her, as Lothan knew, but it concealed an entirely different nature.

Once he had seen the amulet, he had considered contacting Midnight and earning the reward, but the talisman itself proved too great a temptation. If Midnight simply lifted the amulet, then Lothan would have no further opportunity to examine it. *For all the good it has done me,* he thought glumly. Despite numerous opportunities to handle the amulet and to scrutinize the interaction between the amulet and Kellan as she wielded mana, he was no closer to unraveling the item's secrets than when he first saw it. Now Midnight knew about it, which he knew would happen eventually. If he had seen it, he was sure other people Midnight had contacted regarding the amulet had also seen it.

But what was Midnight's angle? That was what Lothan couldn't understand. The amulet was within Midnight's grasp, yet not only did Kellan still have it, but Midnight was supposedly working with her on this shadowrun. Lothan had no doubt the elf could have snatched the amulet if she wanted to. The fact she hadn't done so suggested there was some reason for leaving it in Kellan's possession—probably the same reason Midnight was ingratiating herself with his apprentice. Was it the connection between Kellan and the amulet? Was it something Midnight hadn't foreseen?

Lothan poured himself a mug of tea and idly stirred some honey into it, savoring the aroma and blowing on it before gingerly sipping the brew. He allowed the warmth and the taste to spread through him before returning to his study. He'd look again for references that might contain a clue to the nature of Kellan's little treasure. Lothan had done his best to warn Kellan about the risks she was taking. The rest was up to her.

Lothan wasn't the only one having a sleepless night. Jackie Ozone was working late hours, putting together pieces of a puzzle that formed a disturbing picture. Tracing Kellan's movements in the metroplex took some effort, but because Jackie had helped Kellan set up many of her resources since she'd come to Seattle, she had an edge. To most deckers, Kellan Colt was just another ghost in the machine, hidden in the shadows. To her friend and associate Jackie Ozone, she was at least visible.

She'd assumed Kellan would abandon the whole idea of the run after being told Squeak's data was useless. It should have been that simple. Jackie didn't count on Kellan being so stubborn, or on Squeak turning up dead. That was what bothered Jackie the most: not that Squeak was dead, but that someone thought it was worth killing him. And that they killed him in such a way that it was obvious Squeak's death was no accident or random act of violence.

Kellan thought it was poison. That suggested a professional hit, but who arranged it? Jackie thought she knew, and her conclusion worried her. She would expect her contact to tie up any loose ends, and if she hadn't sanctioned this particular clean-up operation, Zhade might have taken it upon himself to deal with the warez dood. Jackie had no doubt the toxic shaman was capable of snuffing out a life without a second thought. And ultimately, that was the problem. What happened if Zhade crossed paths with Kellan and decided *she* was an obstacle? No, not if. *When* they crossed paths, which they would, since Kellan was hell-bent on going on this run.

She sighed, pushing her cyberdeck away and leaning back to massage her temples, trying to soothe away the persistent headache she'd developed. Not mentioning Kellan's involvement was supposed to keep her out of harm's way! But Kellan was putting together a team anyway. Jackie had turned down the run, and G-Dogg and Liada had turned down the run, but they couldn't refuse Kellan's requests for help in setting it up.

So, what was she going to do? If she did nothing, Kellan and her team would have to deal with Zhade sooner or later, along with anyone else her employer decided to hire for this run. On the other hand, if Jackie told her employer about Kellan's involvement, they were likely to deal with her the same way they dealt with Squeak to make sure she didn't become another loose end. *Damned if I do, damned if I don't.*

If she couldn't prevent Kellan from taking on the run, at least she could try to keep her safe. She could make life a little harder for Zhade and, if she played her cards right, nobody would know she had anything to do with it. Jackie called up her address book with a thought and flicked through the menu, selecting a number. In an instant, she was connected.

"Hey, Stella," she said when her contact answered. "How would you like to come out on top of a smuggler for once?"

"What the frag happened?"

Crash glanced away, then met his leader's glare.

"She was a mage," he said. "She hit us with some spell. . . ."

"But not before she was already out the door!" came the angry retort. "You had time to off her!"

"She had a gun in my—" Keefer protested.

"Shut up! I don't want to hear it."

The Brain Eaters lapsed into silence for a moment. Their leader, a big troll called Boot, continued to fume. He was hacked off by the news of Squeak's sudden demise, but he was furious that four members of his gang had been rousted by the *chica* who did it, who then jandered off like they were nothing.

"Who the frag is this slitch?" he growled to nobody in particular, pacing in front of the bank of trid- and flatscreens on one wall of the Brain Eaters' doss in Redmond.

"We don't know," Crash said, answering for the others, who were too intimidated to speak. Several other gang members lounged around, alternately amused by the chewing out and glad they weren't the focus of Boot's anger.

"I want you to find out!" the troll shot back, stomping to a halt in front of Crash. "I want a name, and then I want her dead! *Nobody* frags with the Brain Eaters and gets away with it. Nobody—"

He broke off at the sound of a muffled protest, followed by the dull thud of a body hitting the unyielding concrete floor. The Brain Eaters turned almost as one toward the front of their hangout, some of them reaching for weapons, as a figure dressed in synthleathers and a tattered plastic slicker stepped through the doorway.

"Oh dear," he smirked, twisting his scarred face into a hideous mask. "Have I come at a bad time?"

"Who the frag are you?" Boot sneered, looking the intruder up and down.

135

"I'm called Zhade, and I've heard some things you might find interesting."

Boot waved off the other Brain Eaters, and they stepped back, tensed hands moving away from their weapons but eyes still focused on the intruder, alert for any sign of trouble. Zhade spread his hands apart to show he was unarmed.

"What've you got?" the gang leader demanded.

"Your boys got their heads handed to them by some girl," Zhade grinned, and Boot gritted his teeth. Word was all over the Barrens already. "I hear one of them got kacked, too."

"So? What the frag do you care?"

"I don't," Zhade said with a shrug, "but I figured you might want to know more about this girl and where you can find her."

"Tell me," Boot grated, and Zhade held up a finger.

"Not so fast. I can help you deal with this problem before it gets any worse. But I want something in return." A hellish red light glowed in the depths of his eyes, and Zhade smiled broadly when the Brain Eaters flinched away from him at the realization that he was a spell-slinger.

Boot just returned Zhade's smile, revealing several gold-capped teeth in his wide mouth. He reached up, adjusted the red fez perched on top of his head, and adopted his best negotiating posture.

"All right," he said. "Let's talk."

11

Orion's phone rang six times before he answered it.
" 'Lo?"

"Rise and shine, chummer," Kellan replied cheer-fully as she shouldered her bag and headed out the door.

"Kellan?" Orion asked in a somewhat confused tone. "What the frag time is it?"

"Time to do some biz, assuming you were serious when you said you would back me up on a run."

That seemed to wake Orion up. "Yeah . . . yeah, of course I was serious," he said. "You got something?"

"Meet me at Flavor in about an hour and you can decide for yourself."

"Okay, I'll be there."

Kellan snapped her phone shut and slipped it into a pocket of her jacket. Things were off to a start. Soon, there would be no turning back.

The little cafe called Flavor was on the outskirts of

Tarislar, the elven district. It served a wide variety of herbal teas and some light vegetarian meals. A small cooperative of local elves ran it, and turned a reasonable profit from both local customers and people from uptown looking for "exotic elven cuisine" and an experience on the edges of the Barrens. The interior of the place was decorated in hand-finished wood beams and columns carved with entwining vines and leaves. They complemented the profusion of potted plants placed strategically throughout the shop. Tall windows let in the sun, which today decided to show itself in favor of the thick gray pall of clouds, smoke and ash often hanging over Puyallup.

Kellan found Orion waiting for her in a booth when she arrived. She ordered a cup of hot tea and grabbed one of the warm rolls from the basket in the middle of the table, savoring its smell as she broke it open and took a bite. Though she'd clearly woken him up with her call, Kellan saw that Orion looked completely awake now, sipping from a steaming mug he cradled in front of him on the polished wood table.

"So you've got something," the elf said. It wasn't a question, given their previous discussion.

"Oh, yeah," Kellan said around a mouthful of bread. She paused for a moment when the waitress brought her tea, then she launched into a description of the past day's events for Orion, chewing as she explained. She told him about her initial meeting with Squeak, the data he discovered, and the warez dood's subsequent mysterious death. For the moment, she left out her meeting with Midnight, and Lothan's misgivings about the elven shadowrunner.

Orion listened carefully to everything Kellan had to say, drinking his tea and eating a roll. When she finished, he set down his mug and rubbed his chin thoughtfully.

"So, you think this kid's data is legit?"

"It has to be," Kellan said. "Why else would someone kack him for it?"

Orion shrugged. "Could have been killed for a lot of reasons," he said. "If this guy was tight with the Brain Eaters, well, gangs have enemies." As a former gang member, Orion knew it better than most.

"Gangers didn't off him," Kellan said with conviction.

"Probably not," Orion agreed. It wasn't like gangs to use poison as a weapon. "It could have been someone else, but that would be a pretty big coincidence. Like you said, if somebody considers this data worth killing for . . ."

Kellan nodded. "Then it has to be worth something, right?"

"Yeah. So what's the plan?"

"Then you're in?" Kellan asked, and Orion smiled.

"Let's say I'm interested and I want to hear more. What's the plan?"

"We go into NAN territory, locate the stash and figure out what's there. Once we know that, I've got an interested buyer and we can negotiate price."

"We?" Orion asked. "So you've already got a team put together?"

"Not yet, but I've got some leads. You can help me out with that part, if you want."

"And what's this job pay?" Orion asked. Kellan knew that he was in, but there were certain formalities to observe.

"Even split of the take," she said. "Minus expenses."

"How big a team?"

"Dunno yet, but no more than five."

Orion nodded in agreement with that number. "Okay," he said after a pause. "Count me in."

"Great," Kellan said. "The next thing we need to do is put together the rest of the team and set up a meet. You up for that?"

"Just point the way," the elf said. "Who do you have in mind?"

"I got a few names from G-Dogg, and I already know one other runner who's interested. She goes by Midnight."

"Midnight?" Orion asked, raising one eyebrow. "I've heard of her. She's pretty high-class—how'd you get her on board?"

"I have my ways," Kellan said with a pleased smile. "I've set up meets with a few other possibilities." She flipped open her phone to show Orion the screen. He glanced at the addresses and times displayed there.

"Looks good," he said. "Let's do it."

*   *   *

The so-called Elven District near the southern shore of Lake Union was what most Seattleites thought an "elven neighborhood" should look like. Whereas Tarislar was filled with derelict and abandoned buildings covered in a fine layer of ash from Mount Rainier, the Elven District was home to brick-front townhouses and renovated nineteenth- and twentieth-century buildings. Ivy grew in profusion across many of the buildings, and there were murals painted by metahuman artists. The whole neighborhood had an artsy, bohemian feel to it, carefully planned to attract both tourists and locals interested in elven culture.

Orion hated the place. From the moment they parked their motorcycles and began walking down the pedestrian-only streets, he insisted on pointing out to Kellan all of the Elven District's flaws, starting with the genetically modified strains of ivy and continuing with the murals, the "traditional" elven and dwarf architecture, and the shops filled with "handmade elven crafts."

"Yeah, handmade in little faerie tree houses," he sneered. "More likely made in Tsimshian or Hong Kong by underpaid child labor."

"It's just drek for the tourists," Kellan said, in an attempt to pacify him.

Orion snorted. "Most of them think Tir Tairngire is like faerieland or something, and Seattle has the exclusive trade agreement."

He continued his rant by moving on to racial stereotypes, and only stopped talking because he was struck momentarily speechless when Kellan stopped in front of a shop and indicated it was the address she had displayed on her phone.

"You have *got* to be kidding me," Orion muttered, looking up at the shop's carved wooden placard. It showed a sword and hammer crossed above an anvil, with the name MITHRIL ARTS arcing above it in pseudorunic script.

"What?" Kellan asked.

"Tradfant," Orion spat, as if that explained everything. When Kellan gave him a quizzical look, he continued. "This place caters to people who expect metahumans to be like something out of a fantasy novel. You know, elves all in flowing gossamer, carrying bows, dwarfs wearing furs and chain mail and saying drek like 'By my father's beard!' It's all a bunch of fraggin' racist tourist crap. The worst thing is that some *metahumans* actually buy into this drek." He threw up his hands in frustration. "It's the traditional fantasy types who make it so nobody can see metas as normal people."

"Well, this is the address the guy gave me," Kellan said. "So behave yourself, okay?"

Orion sighed. "Fine. But I don't know what kind of talent you expect to find in here."

A bell jangled as Kellan opened the door to the shop. It was like stepping into the past, or onto a set for a simsense production. Or maybe the props department of a simflick. The inside of the shop was paneled in rough-hewn wood, also used for the shelving and the counter running along one side. Racks and display cases held swords, daggers, axes and other medieval weapons. Some were beautifully detailed, others much more functional looking. There were heavy shirts of fine chain links ranging in sizes from dwarf to one displayed on a troll-sized mannequin, which dominated the back corner. Armored greaves, gauntlets, breastplates and a profusion of helmets took up the rest of the display space.

The curtains in the doorway to the back of the shop parted and a dwarf woman emerged. She wore what looked like a medieval peasant costume: a puffy-sleeved blouse and a long, homespun-looking dress with a full bodice laced up the front. Her light brown hair was long but caught up in braids wound at the nape of her neck. She favored Kellan and Orion with a wide smile and a twinkle in her brown eyes.

"Hello there!" she said. "Welcome to Mithril Arts. Can I help you?"

Kellan did her best not to snicker at the pained expression on Orion's face. "We're looking for Draven," she told the woman.

"Of course," she said. "He's in the back." She nodded toward the curtained door. "Go right ahead, he's expecting you." Then she bustled off behind the counter.

Kellan led the way through the doorway, pushing aside the curtain. The space behind the shop was a combination of storeroom and workshop. It included an old-fashioned forge, complete with anvil, hammer, tongs and other tools of the blacksmith's art. The forge was cold today, but a dwarf was sitting on a low stool beside a workbench. He was linking metal rings together to make a shirt of mail, twisting and crimping them with a set of pliers and deft movements of his large hands. He glanced up from his work as the two shadowrunners entered.

"Right on time," the dwarf said, glancing at the analog cuckoo clock hanging on the wall. "Come in, come in." He set aside the mail and began clearing off a couple of the nearby stools.

"You're Draven?" Kellan asked, and the dwarf nodded vigorously.

"That's me," he said. "Have yourself a seat and let's talk business."

Kellan studied Draven as she and Orion settled in next to the burly dwarf. Like his entire race, Draven was built wide and low to the ground. Kellan estimated he was about a meter and a half tall—average for a dwarf. He was barrel-chested, with wide shoulders and arms thickly corded with muscle. He wore a tee-shirt that stretched across his chest, and a pair of faded jeans under an old leather apron. Heavy work boots covered his feet. He had a thick mane of brown hair, receding somewhat in front, and a full, bristling beard. His hair was braided into a thick ponytail that stretched down his back. The portions of his face not covered in hair were craggy and deeply lined. He was older than Kellan expected—at least twice her age, she guessed. Still, his bulging muscles showed he was in excellent shape, and a few scars, white against his tanned skin, showed that Draven was a dwarf with experience.

"Can I get you anything?" he asked. "Maybe a little something to drink?" He had a trace of an accent Kellan couldn't identify. It sounded vaguely Scottish or English.

"No thanks," she said, and Draven nodded.

"You wouldn't mind if I had a drop?" When Kellan shrugged, Draven took a flask from the workbench, popped the top and belted back a deep gulp before replacing the stopper and wiping the back of his hand across his mouth.

"Well, then, let's get down to business," he said. "You told me you're looking to make a little trip out of town, eh?"

"That's right," Kellan said.

"Delivering or picking up?" Draven asked. "Or is it both?"

"Picking up," Kellan told him, "or at the minimum, checking out a location." She briefly explained the run.

The dwarf nodded. "There's the potential for a good haul?"

"A *very* good haul, and everyone gets a share."

Draven's bushy beard split into a smile. "An' just how much potential are we talkin' about here?"

"We won't know for sure until we get there," Kellan told him, "but it's a lot of potential, if I'm right."

"And a fair amount of wasted time and effort if you're wrong."

"I'm not," Kellan said.

Draven paused for a moment. "Well, you're certainly sure of yourself, I'll give you that. I can see why Lothan decided to take you on."

"You know Lothan?" Kellan asked, and Draven chuckled.

"Of *course* I know Lothan," he said. "He and I were working the shadows before you were even a twinkle in your daddy's eye. I take it he either doesn't know about this particular opportunity of yours or doesn't much care for it. Which is it?"

"He's not interested," Kellan said. Would that kill Draven's interest as well?

"Well, Lothan likes to play it safe these days," Draven mused. "He was quite the daredevil in his younger days, though, let me tell you!"

"You still seem pretty daring yourself," Kellan replied, and Draven smiled.

"Ah, if only you'd known me twenty years ago," he said. "Still, I can't afford to play it quite as safe as Lothan does these days. You have to take risks if you want to find the really big score, eh?" He gave Kellan a wink and slapped his leather-covered thigh with one hand. "All right then, Kellan, if you say this opportunity of yours is worth the effort, then I'm willing to give it a chance."

"Great," Kellan said. "We're meeting tonight to

outline the plan." She gave Draven the place and time, and the old dwarf nodded.

"I'll be there," he said.

Kellan didn't speak again until they were out of earshot of the shop.

"Well?" she asked Orion. He remained silent for a bit longer, hands jammed into the pockets of his jacket, then shrugged.

"You sure he can still cut it?"

"G-Dogg seemed to think so."

"G-Dogg didn't exactly give you his A-list, did he?" the elf observed.

"He wouldn't have given me runners who couldn't do the job," she countered.

"Well, I guess we'll find out. Let's hope this next guy is a more impressive prospect, though."

12

Tukwila was in the southern downtown area, not
far from the Seattle-Tacoma International Airport,
so it didn't take them long to travel there. Lone Star
did a good job of patrolling I-5 during the daylight
hours, especially close to downtown and the airport,
so they managed to avoid any trouble with go-gangs.
Tukwila, on the other hand, was considered the
roughest neighborhood in the area. It made Columbia look upscale, though it was a far cry from the
lawlessness of the Redmond or Puyallup Barrens.
Needless to say, Lone Star didn't put much effort
into keeping Tukwila safe for the SINners.

The address Kellan had been given was a bar that
was just as run-down as the rest of the neighborhood.
It was a one-story building with peeling white paint,
and heavy steel mesh protecting the windows. Weeds
sprouted up from cracks in the pavement, choking
parts of the parking lot. The lot was empty. In fact,

according to the faded sign on the door, the place wasn't even open for another hour.

Kellan tried the door and found it unlocked, so she pushed it open and stepped inside, followed closely by Orion.

"We're not open yet!" called a voice from the other side of the room. Kellan could see a swarthy man wearing a stained apron, with his shirtsleeves rolled up. He set a cardboard box on the top of the bar, glaring in their direction from under heavy black brows.

"It's okay, Lou," another voice said. "They're here to see me."

This voice came from the back corner of the bar, and the speaker stood as he spoke, setting a half-empty glass of beer on the table. He was tall for a human, and his rough-hewn features and erect posture gave him a strong presence. He had a prominent nose, sharp cheekbones and a coppery complexion that contrasted with raven dark hair, worn long in a single braid down his back. He was dressed in a flannel shirt with the sleeves rolled up, unbuttoned at the collar. He wore a white thermal shirt underneath, and a necklace of carved bone. Both shirts were tucked into a pair of faded jeans, in turn tucked into laced-up moccasin boots.

As Kellan appraised him, his dark eyes regarded her. Whatever his opinion, his face remained as impassive as stone.

"Natokah," he said by way of introduction, confirming he was the man they had come to meet.

"I'm Kellan," she said. "We talked. This is Orion."

Natokah nodded acknowledgement and gestured for them to sit. Once they were all seated he said matter-of-factly, "You are planning a foray into Native territory. You will need a guide, and an intermediary to speak with the spirits of the land—though I see both of you have your own capabilities."

Interesting. Kellan knew Natokah was a shaman. She'd hoped to have access to his expertise when she contacted him off G-Dogg's list. Obviously, he'd noticed her and Orion's magical talents.

"We can handle ourselves," Kellan said modestly, "but we're not experienced in dealing with spirits from the native lands."

"I am," Natokah replied. "*Very* experienced. Where do you plan to go?"

"Salish-Shidhe territory," Kellan replied. "Recon the target site and return with information on what's there."

"And what do you expect to find there?"

"Something to make the trip worthwhile," Kellan countered.

Natokah offered a faint smile in return. "So you're not sure," he said.

"If we were sure, there wouldn't be any need to go."

"What's the payment?"

"Some cred up front and a share of the profits," Kellan told him. She quoted a figure and Natokah remained silent for a moment.

"That's not much," he said.

"That's just an advance," Kellan said. "The rest is on completion."

"How much?"

"As much as we can get."

"Split how many ways?"

"Five, if everything goes well," Kellan told him.

"Fewer, if it doesn't," Natokah responded. There was a moment of silence, then the shaman nodded. "All right," he said. "I'm interested."

"Good. We're—"

"Hey, you're not allowed—" Lou's voice shouted, then was cut off by a loud "Urk!" and a crashing sound. Instantly, the three shadowrunners were on their feet as a group of gang members wearing black and white poured into the bar from the kitchen entrance. They each wore a red fez topped with a gold tassel and carried various implements of violence. In the lead were Crash and the ork she'd run into at Squeak's apartment.

"Colt!" Crash yelled, pointing at Kellan. "You're dead meat!" Natokah leaned toward Kellan.

"Seems like you could use a trip out of the plex right now," he commented wryly, then the gangers charged.

There were a half-dozen Brain Eaters, including Keefer and Zoog, armed with knives, hand razors or heavy lengths of chain. The ork carried a heavy wooden bat like a club. Two of them had visible cybereyes, their normal eyes replaced with solid silver spheres with no iris or pupil.

Kellan kicked her chair into Crash's path as Orion's sword cleared its sheath in a flash of metal. As the Brain Eater tripped over the chair, Kellan reached for the stun baton inside her jacket. The close quarters made casting a spell too risky. Besides, most of the spells Kellan knew tended to involve things exploding, and she didn't want to wreck the bar. A pistol wasn't too useful in close quarters, especially in the midst of friendly targets.

With a twist of his blade, Orion brushed aside the bat his opponent was swinging at his head. Then he spun and buried his sword in the next Brain Eater's stomach, causing him to howl in pain. The elf yanked his sword free, sending the ganger stumbling backward and doing his level best to hold his guts in as he bled all over the floor.

Crash only stumbled over Kellan's chair, keeping his feet under him, but she had her stun baton in hand by then. Scalpel-like blades gleamed at the ganger's fingertips, but her weapon gave Kellan the advantage of greater reach. As Crash lunged at her, she wielded the stun baton like a short sword, making a lightning-fast thrust at his torso. The tip of the weapon connected and there was a loud crack as hundreds of volts slammed into the ganger's body. He stiffened and dropped to lie twitching on the floor.

Natokah ducked under the chain swung at him and hooked a leg out to sweep the Brain Eater off his feet. The ganger tumbled backward, losing his grip on his weapon as he tried unsuccessfully to break his fall. The shaman's voice rang out with an ululating cry that seemed to reverberate in the confines of the bar.

Orion met Zoog head-on. A slightly curved blade emerged from the back of the Brain Eater's wrist, about the length of his forearm, tapering to a needle-sharp point. He swung the razor-edged spur at the elf, who blocked it gracefully with his blade. Orion held the sword hilt-up, blade pointing at the floor. As he blocked past his left shoulder, he just as quickly reversed it, bringing the sword down in an overhand arc. The Brain Eater dived to the side to avoid it.

"Watch out!" Kellan yelled, as another of the gangers closed in on Orion, coming to help Zoog. A flash of Orion's double-edged blade held his second opponent at bay for the moment. Kellan lunged in at the second ganger, jamming the stun baton into his side. He jerked as it discharged, but his heavy synthleather jacket must have insulated him from some of the shock, since he stayed on his feet.

Orion's sword had left a bleeding gash along Zoog's arm, cutting through his heavy leathers like tissue paper. The ganger cursed and came at the elf again, but was blocked by another twist of his blade.

Natokah's chant rose into a shrieking call and Kellan felt the crackle of magical power in the air. She turned to see the shaman raise his hands, his fingers taking on the appearance of hooked claws. There was a sharp cast to his features, like the profile of some predatory bird. The floorboards of the bar groaned, like some great creature had been roused from a deep sleep.

The Brain Eaters hesitated at the sound, and the shadowrunners stood ready for a renewed attack. Natokah slowly lowered his hands, and his features returned to normal as a strong breeze blew through the bar, carrying a swirl of drink napkins into the air. Kellan realized there were no open windows or doors that could account for the wind inside. Then smoke seemed to condense out of the air between the gangers and the shadowrunners. It took on a humanoid shape, and then solidified into the form of an ork. He was dressed in heavy work boots, jeans and a button-down shirt with the sleeves rolled up over his bulging forearms. He had a heavy apron tied over his clothes and balanced a thick cudgel on his shoulder.

"I think you should be leaving here . . . now," the ork rumbled in a deep bass, glaring at the Brain Eaters. "Or do I have to see you out myself?" He tapped the cudgel against his open palm for emphasis.

Crash staggered to his feet, simultaneously recovering from the effects of Kellan's stun baton and his initial shock at the ork's sudden appearance. Rather than back down, he rushed the ork, slashing at him with his hand razors. The ork stood his ground, blocking the attack with an almost casual gesture from his cudgel. Then he shoved the Brain Eater back, wound up, and swung.

The sickening sound of wood striking flesh and

bone echoed in the small room. The blow spun Crash halfway around before he crumpled in a heap on the floor. The other gangers looked in horror from the smiling ork to their chummer and back again.

"Anyone else want a piece of this?" the ork roared, taking a step forward. The gangers shrank back from him. "Get out of here! Now!" he yelled, and the Brain Eaters scrambled to gather up their fallen comrades. They retreated from the bar with only brief backward glances. When they were gone, the ork turned to Natokah.

"Thank you, my friend," the shaman said with a slight bow.

The ork waved it off. "My pleasure. Fraggin' gangers—don't need them causing trouble around here. Hey, Lou!" he called. "You're doin' a good job! Just make sure to pour me one once in a while, okay?" The dumbfounded bartender could only nod in agreement. The ork saluted Natokah with a wave and then dissolved into the same cloud of smoke from which he'd appeared. In an instant, he was gone.

"Who was that?" Kellan asked.

"The spirit of this place," the shaman replied. "Its hearth, its living essence. I called upon his help." He turned to Lou, who had approached the group with a bemused expression. "Leave a glass of whiskey, neat, over the bar tonight, and once during the week of each full moon," he told him. "It will appease his thirst and keep him happy."

A smile split the bartender's stubbled face. "I will," he said. "Thanks! You guys are welcome here anytime." Then he retreated back to the bar.

"Yeah, thanks," Orion told Natokah, "but I could have handled them."

The shaman smiled. "I'm sure you could have."

"So," the shaman said, turning toward Kellan. "I think you were saying something about getting together later?"

13

They met that night at Kellan's place. Her apartment wasn't large, but there was room enough for them to sprawl across Kellan's secondhand furniture and discuss the specifics of the run. Kellan made introductions for those who hadn't already met, and it seemed clear to her some of the runners had at least heard of each other. Midnight and Natokah in particular seemed to know each other by reputation, though they gave no indication they had met.

Draven showed up at the door wearing a chain mail shirt over a lining of ballistic armor, with a double-bladed axe strapped at his side. The topper, literally, was the horned helmet on the dwarf's head, adding at least another twenty centimeters to his height. Kellan could tell that, despite looking like a prop from a fantasy sim, the helmet was equipped with some communications and targeting gear. She was also willing to bet the axe was a modern composite, and not hammer-forged iron. Though Orion rolled his eyes at the sight of the dwarf, he managed to hold his tongue, for which Kellan was grateful. There was no need to start things off on the wrong foot. If anyone else took exception to Draven's tradfant getup, they showed no sign of it.

Once everyone was there, Kellan got right down to business.

"The run is fairly simple," she said. "A trip out of the plex into Salish-Shidhe Council territory to a specific location. It's strictly an information-gathering job: we go, we see what's there, get all the data we can, and get back home, all without alerting the border patrols or the SSC security forces."

"What exactly are we supposed to be scouting?" Natokah asked.

"I'm not prepared to share that information at this point," Kellan said, trying to be diplomatic.

The shaman's dark eyes focused on her for a long moment.

"We're all professionals here," Natokah finally said, spreading his hands to include everyone in the room. "If you're not willing to show us a level of trust, why should we do the same?"

Kellan leaned forward as she responded. "I don't consider this to be a question of trust. As professional shadowrunners, you don't always get to know all the details going into a run. That's the team leader's responsibility, and I'm the team leader. If you can't work within the terms of the job, the door's over there."

All eyes went to Natokah. The shaman's face was inscrutable as he eyed Kellan.

"We'll play it your way for now."

Kellan looked at the other runners, but no one else voiced any objections.

"Good," she said. She wasn't sure she managed to keep her relief out of her voice. "The first thing we need to do is get from here to there, which means leaving the metroplex and crossing over into NAN territory without raising any red flags."

"I can help with that," Draven volunteered. "I know smugglers who work the routes south and east of here. They run cargo—and sometimes passengers—in and out of NAN territory, from Seattle down to Denver and back."

"If I give you the general location, can you arrange for transportation in and out of the SSC territories?"

Draven nodded. "The closest city should be enough," he said. "I assume we'd need to be on our own from there?"

"Right," Kellan replied. "Okay," she manipulated the controls of a flatscreen datapad before setting it on the low table in the middle of the room. "This is our target area in the SSC. It looks like Lewiston-Clarkston is the closest city."

Draven looked over the map. "That should be enough to go on," he said. "It's not far off the major smuggling routes, so I should be able to find us a t-bird pilot willing to take a short side trip."

"How would we leave the plex?" Orion asked,

leaning in to look at the map. Kellan doubted the elf had ever been outside of Seattle. From what she knew, Orion had grown up on the streets of Puyallup. Though many people associated elves with the Awakened wilderness, this elf had probably never even seen a real forest, much less hiked through one.

"Our departure point will be up to the smuggler," Natokah interjected, "but my guess is we'll go through the Puyallup Barrens. I know of several places there where we can make the crossing."

Kellan nodded. "As long as there is minimal chance of anyone else catching wind of this."

"Of course. The people I know are discreet," Draven replied.

"Well," Orion commented, "If we're headed out into NAN land, we're going to need wilderness gear, right?"

"Some of that we can acquire in Lewiston or the nearby area, I imagine," Natokah said. "The less cargo we bring with us out of the metroplex, the easier it will be."

"Plus, if we're carrying out a lot of wilderness gear, it gives anyone who's watching an idea of what we're doing," Midnight added. She was lounging in one of Kellan's beat-up easy chairs. "Better to find what we need closer to our objective."

"I'm not ashamed to say I've never been camping in my life," Orion stated. "But it seems like we've got a lot of muscle just to go out in the woods."

He glanced somewhat pointedly at Draven. Natokah spoke up before Kellan could answer.

"It's a wise precaution," he said. "The Awakening affected animals as well as people, and there's no telling what we might run into in the wild. There are also spirits—some mischievous, others more dangerous."

"That's going to be your department," Kellan told the shaman. She suddenly wished she had time to return to Lothan for a more detailed course in summoning and controlling spirits. "You guys," she said to Orion and Draven, "deal with anything else that gets in our way. Midnight handles security." Natokah glanced briefly at the infiltration expert, a thoughtful look on his face.

Let him wonder why we need a security specialist along, Kellan thought. She was glad the shaman had chosen to stick with the run. She had confidence in her own magical abilities, but Natokah knew the sorts of spirits they might encounter outside the metroplex. And he obviously had knowledge of the Native American Nations that surely would be useful. All Kellan knew about the NAN came from what she learned in school, and secondhand stories and rumors. She passed through NAN territory to get from Kansas City to Seattle, but you didn't learn a lot about a place by riding through it. Natokah was a valuable resource.

Still, Kellan had been serious when she told him he could walk. The shaman was within his rights to try to get more information about the run, but she had just as much of a right to deny him. This run was her opportunity to call the shots. If Natokah or anyone else had a problem with that, then Kellan didn't need them. She felt she'd handled things pretty well. She had a good feeling about this run.

"I've got a bad feeling about this," Orion said later, after everyone else had left. There'd been some additional discussion of equipment needed and the timing of the run, then Kellan had given everyone their up-front share of the cred and sent them on their way. Now they had to wait until Draven arranged transportation out of the metroplex, which he seemed to think he could set up fairly quickly.

"Why?" Kellan asked Orion, as he stared out the window into the darkness.

The elf gave a little snort of mirthless laughter. "Don't you ever feel just a little overwhelmed?" he asked, turning away from the window. "Maybe it's just the idea of leaving the metroplex. Maybe it's just that it seems like things are happening pretty fast."

"Yeah, I feel that way too," she replied. "But things're working out. Pretty soon this run will be over and we'll have some real cred to show for it."

"I hope so. Nice the way you handled Natokah, by the way," he said.

"Thanks. But I'm glad he decided to stay. I think he's going to be a big asset on this run."

Orion nodded. "Yeah, he seems to know his stuff.

And that business with the hearth spirit was pretty impressive. All the same, I'd keep an eye on him—on all of them—if I were you."

"I don't know," Kellan replied. "I think Natokah and Draven are trustworthy enough. They don't seem to have a lot of ambition beyond the next run. Natokah in particular seems like an honorable enough guy. But you're right, I probably should keep an eye on them both."

"And Midnight, too," Orion reminded her. "You can't trust her any more than Draven or Natokah."

"You're not the first one to think that," Kellan said. "Lothan showed up here the other night to give me the same warning."

"What did he say?"

"Typical Lothan stuff. He just gave me this mysterious warning, no details, like I'm supposed to trust *him*."

"Don't you?" Orion asked. "I mean, I know you don't agree with him about everything . . ." Kellan remembered that Orion didn't know the full extent of her dealings—her double-dealings—with Lothan. She'd kept the fact that he was working for the opposition on the Ares run a secret from everyone else involved in the "asset acquisition."

She shrugged, choosing to sidestep the question. "I think she'll be useful on this run. Besides," she glanced up at Orion from her place on the couch, "she says she knew my mom."

"Really?"

Kellan nodded. "Yeah. She recognized this," she said, touching her amulet. "Said it belonged to a shadowrunner named Mustang she used to run with, someone who taught her the ropes. She always wondered what happened to her. She says I look a lot like her, and the timing is right for her to have been my mother."

"You sure she's on the level?" Orion asked. He sat on the other end of the couch. "I mean, she could just be telling you this to get in good with you for some reason."

"What reason? She didn't even know I was looking for information about my mother," Kellan said. "She brought it up. I guess she could be making it up, but the stuff she said about my mom fits the little I know."

"Does she know what happened to your mom?"

Kellan shook her head. "No, she says she lost track of her. It seems like she wants to know what happened almost as much as I do. It's not much, but it's a start. Midnight really seems to want to help me out, like my mom helped her. I think I can trust her as much as you can trust anyone in this business."

Orion smiled ruefully. "Well, for what it's worth," he said, "I trust you."

Kellan was surprised. "Really?" she asked.

He nodded. "Yeah, really. You took a big risk coming to me when you found out the Ancients were being set up. You didn't really know anything about me, but you took a chance in order to do what you thought was right. People just don't do that for each other, especially in our line of work. That's how I know I can trust you."

"Thanks," Kellan said quietly. "I trust you, too." There was a moment when Kellan was caught in the earnest look in Orion's green eyes. Then he glanced away and an awkward pause hung in the air.

"Well then, we've each got somebody in the biz we can trust. Look, I should get going," he said. "Give me a buzz when we're set to go, or if you need anything else, okay?" He stood up from the couch, grabbing his leather jacket from the back of a chair and slipping it on.

"Sure," Kellan said. "No problem."

"Catch you later," he said, pulling open the door.

"Okay. And, Orion?"

"Yeah?"

"Thanks," Kellan said.

"Null sheen," the elf replied. "G'night." Then he was out the door and it closed quietly behind him.

Kellan sat on her couch, hugging her knees to her chest and thinking. Events were in motion. Now it was just a matter of finding out if Squeak's data was the gold mine he'd thought it was. Just a trip out into foreign territory, through hostile Awakened wilderness, in search of something that someone else was willing to kill for. "Nothing to it," Kellan muttered to herself, glad she appeared so confident to Orion. She hoped everyone else on the team saw the same thing as he did.

She'd been truly surprised, and deeply honored, by Orion's declaration of trust. Their mutual trust was based on mutual respect. She'd gone out on a limb for Orion and he'd done the same, getting thrown out of the Ancients go-gang for defying its leader, Green Lucifer. He could have just kept his mouth shut, could have ignored Kellan's information that said the gang was being double-crossed. Since then, she had learned Orion did what he believed was right, and she trusted him to do the right thing.

Could she say the same about anyone else on the team? Not really. The other shadowrunners she knew acted out of self-interest. Sometimes it was enlightened self-interest, but more often it was just looking out for number one. A few runners followed a personal code, but it seemed like everyone held things back. Everyone had a hidden agenda. Maybe that was another reason she trusted Orion: the elf warrior certainly didn't hold anything back. He was as direct as a sword thrust about pretty much everything. There were no secrets, and she could rely on him to tell her exactly what he thought.

Kellan picked up her phone and pulled up a number from the menu, tucking her feet underneath her on the couch. When the voice mail system answered, she paused for only a second before leaving a message.

"Midnight, it's Kellan. Give me a call in the morning. We need to talk."

14

Kellan arranged to meet Midnight the following afternoon. She loved the nocturnal lifestyle, for which shadowrunners were famous, as much as the next guy, but this daytime meeting seemed appropriate since she wanted to clear away some shadows. Midnight had agreed to come back to Kellan's place—this wasn't a conversation Kellan wanted to have in public, and she felt a little stronger on her own turf. It was the same reason she'd decided to bring the team there last night, even though most runners would consider revealing your home base to anyone to be a rookie mistake.

Midnight called up from the lobby of the building right on time. Kellan buzzed her in, then paced by the door until she knocked.

Midnight wasn't wearing her "working clothes" of form-fitting leather. Instead, she wore a loose fitting leather jacket and a tee-shirt tucked into a pair of jeans worn over black leather boots. A bright red messenger bag was slung over her shoulder, and her long hair fell loose around her shoulders. Out of her usual ponytail, her hair softened the sharp planes and angles of her face. Even dressed so casually, however, Midnight still looked like a model and moved like a dancer as she glided into Kellan's apartment.

"Right on time," Kellan said. "Thanks."

"I want you to know," Midnight said lightly, "getting up during the day isn't something I do for just anybody."

"I feel suitably honored," she quipped, "and I appreciate it."

"Not a problem. Actually, I wanted to talk to you, too."

"Really? What about?" Kellan asked.

"You first."

Kellan gestured toward the same chair Midnight had adorned last night, letting her take off her jacket and settle in before she continued. Kellan sat on the edge of the couch and decided to plunge right into it.

"I want to know what you and Lothan talked about that night at the club."

Midnight didn't bat an eye, but settled more deeply into the chair.

"Have you asked Lothan about it?" she asked.

"Yes, I have," Kellan said. "He wouldn't give me any details, but he doesn't think I should trust you."

To Kellan's surprise, Midnight nodded. "Lothan's no fool, Kellan. There's no reason you *should* trust me, and every reason for you not to. Trusting people in this business is dangerous. You should know that."

"So are you saying you can't be trusted?"

Midnight smiled. "Of course not. I'm the very soul of honor and discretion. You should trust me implicitly in all things."

Kellan laughed. "That's almost exactly what Lothan said when I asked him the same question." Her smiled faded. "I'm serious, Midnight, I need to know."

The elf leaned forward, resting her elbows on her knees, her hands loosely clasped.

"All right," she said. "If it's that important. Honestly, I decided not to say anything before because you're Lothan's student, and your business with him is none of mine. What's between Lothan and me is just business, and I felt a professional obligation to be discreet."

Kellan was taken aback. She felt as if Midnight was chastising her for asking a fellow professional to break confidence. But she really felt like she needed to know what was going on between her teacher and this woman who could be her friend. So she only nodded for Midnight to go on.

"Lothan and I had . . . an arrangement involving you."

"Involving *me*?"

"Indirectly," the elf continued. "Specifically, your amulet."

"What about it?"

169

"I knew that it was the most unique thing Mustang owned," Midnight said. "I figured even if she disappeared, it might turn up sooner or later. If she was in debt, she might sell it to raise some nuyen. If she was dead . . . well, someone else might do the same thing. Even though the chances were slim that I would ever find out what happened, I had to make the effort.

"So I talked to a few people I knew, experts in rare trinkets. I provided a description, asked them to keep an eye out for the amulet, and told them I would pay a finder's fee for anyone with any information about it. One of those experts was Lothan."

"So Lothan knew you were looking for this?" Kellan asked, touching the amulet.

Midnight nodded. "Needless to say, I was rather surprised when I found out about you on my own and discovered you were Lothan's student. I wanted to know why he didn't tell me immediately when he saw you wearing that amulet."

"What did he say?" Kellan asked.

Midnight shrugged. "He said he didn't want you having anything to do with me, that I had nothing to offer, and that you were better off studying with him. Really though, I think once he saw the amulet, Lothan wanted to keep it where he could study it. Maybe he thought I intended to take it from you."

"Or from him," Kellan supplied.

"Maybe," Midnight said. "I don't really know. I know Lothan can be a little controlling when it comes to things that interest him."

"A little?" Kellan asked with a snort of laughter. "Try a lot."

"Maybe he just wanted more of a chance to study the amulet before he told me about it, or he thought he was protecting you because I wanted to steal the amulet from you. After all, he didn't know why I was really looking for it."

"And that's it?"

"That's it. I'm sorry I didn't tell you sooner, Kellan, but I didn't want to cast any doubts on Lothan's motivations."

"Lothan doesn't need any help in that department." Kellan sighed. "Thanks for telling me the truth."

"No problem. I hope it helps."

Kellan nodded.

"Don't be too hard on Lothan," Midnight said. "He's right about one thing: it's difficult and dangerous to trust anyone in this business."

"Yeah, I've noticed," Kellan replied.

"Speaking of not trusting people . . ."

"Yeah?"

"I wanted to talk to you about Natokah," Midnight said. "I have some concerns."

"What kind of concerns?"

Midnight sat back and flapped her hand as she spoke. "About how much we should trust him to handle on this run. Last night, he seemed pretty interested in finding out the destination."

"He backed down about that," Kellan pointed out.

"Yes, and I think you handled him just fine," Midnight replied. "But I did a little checking into his background last night. Most of what I know about Natokah is by reputation—which is mostly good. If we're going to work together, however, I wanted to know a little more."

"What did you find out?" Kellan asked, curious.

"He's from the Sioux Nation, Laramie," Midnight explained. "He belongs to the Navajo tribe. The interesting thing is that there's a warrant out in Sioux territory for his arrest."

"For what?"

"Murder," Midnight said flatly.

Natokah examined the wards protecting his modest rooms in Columbia. Though he'd renewed them recently, it was wise to ensure they remained strong and stable before he engaged in astral travel. When he was satisfied with his inspection, Natokah prepared his working space. He set the telecom to divert any incoming calls to voice mail, dimmed the lights and spread out a brightly colored blanket on a clear space on the floor. He turned on his entertainment system and selected a drumming-music file. Live music would have been more authentic, but a modern shaman made do with what was at hand.

He lit a bundle of sweet white sage, blowing gently on the end of it until it was smoldering. He ritually cleansed his space, signing seals of protection to the four directions and honoring those spirits. He set the sage wand to burn in a shell on the floor next to the blanket. Then he adjusted the volume of the music and lay down on the blanket. He stretched and relaxed, releasing the tension from his muscles, feeling the weight of his body pressing against the floor. The sweet smoke of the sage curled in white wisps overhead. The beat of the drum flowed over him, like the beating of his heart.

Natokah took hold of the drumbeat; let it flow over and through him, leading him into a deep trance. With practiced ease, he closed his eyes, settled his body and relaxed. His awareness of the physical world fell away, and he was floating in a soft, warm and comfortable darkness. Then he opened his eyes.

Natokah saw his body lying on the blanket beneath him. He hovered over it, like the sage smoke passing through and around him. The drumming music faded to a dull background noise. His spirit was outside his body, floating on the astral plane. From here Natokah could see the wards around his apartment as shimmering, ghostly echoes of the physical walls. They were no obstacles to him, as their creator, but to any other spirit intruder, they would be as solid and strong as stone walls. With no more thought than crossing a room, Natokah's spirit flew through the wall of his apartment and out into the air over Seattle.

The shaman had spent time exploring the spirit world around the metroplex, but this time he had a specific destination. Natokah's spirit angled up, flying high over the city toward the east. Then, with the speed of thought, he flew off, leaving Seattle and his physical form far behind. The sky above and the land below became little more than a blur of light and color as Natokah traveled at a speed unequaled by any physical creature, faster than a hawk, eagle or even a dragon.

It took him only moments to cover hundreds of kilometers, and Natokah slowed as he approached a familiar place some distance from the metroplex he currently called home. Outwardly, it was a humble-looking building, a long, low house built of wood. Though constructed using modern techniques, its design honored the style and appearance of native structures dating from before Europeans discovered the Americas. Carvings adorned the trim of the building near the roof and accented the support beams. Those carvings, Natokah knew, served more than a decorative function. Their design was integral to the spirit walls of the building, which he saw as clearly as the wards around his own home. He also saw the guardians of this place, ever watchful, and aware of his arrival.

One spirit stood guard at each wall of the lodge, which were set to face the cardinal directions. They had the shape of people, but wore heavy clothing that showed no bare flesh. Heavy jackets and leggings of hide were trimmed with fringe and beadwork. Soft moccasins covered their feet, and mittens of the finest calfskin covered their hands. Over their faces they each wore an elaborately carved mask depicting a totem animal: bear, eagle, snake and raven. Their true appearances were hidden beneath the masks—assuming the masks were *not* their true appearances. Guardian spirits, summoned and honored to watch over this place.

They knew Natokah, and the eagle guardian nodded acknowledgement to him as he arrived, standing aside so he could enter. The shaman's spirit passed through the wards and the walls of the lodge as though they were no more than smoke.

The room Natokah entered was quite ordinary. A brightly colored blanket, similar to the one his physical body lay upon hundreds of kilometers away, hung on one wall. A desk occupied one corner of the room and held a keyboard and flatscreen monitor. On one wall hung shelves containing a few books and curios, while the opposite corner held a small couch and end table. An old man sat on the couch. He glanced up from the datapad he was reading as Natokah entered.

His hair was long—well past his shoulders—and iron gray. It had been so for as long as Natokah could recall. Two braids framed a strong, lined and weathered face, a face that had seen many momentous events. His eyes were like dark stones and gleamed with insight; his mouth was a hard, strong line. There was no need for Natokah to manifest his presence in the room, since he knew the old man could see him perfectly well. His dark eyes missed very little.

Stephen Kenson

"Your report," he said, gesturing toward the space in front of him.

Natokah folded his legs, sitting in the air just a couple of meters away from the other man.

"Sir, I have made contact with a group of shadowrunners planning a mission into Salish-Shidhe territory. Their objective is somewhere near the Lewiston-Clarkston area."

"Do you know what their objective is?" the old man asked. Natokah shook his head.

"Not yet. The shadowrunner arranging things is keeping that information to herself for the time being. I don't think I will be able to find out the objective before the run begins."

"How do the shadowrunners plan to reach their objective?"

"One of the team is to make arrangements with a smuggler along the eastern routes to get us to the Lewiston area," Natokah replied. "I could arrange for the elimination of the shadowrunners after they have crossed the border."

The old man thought for a moment. "Do you feel this mission is an immediate threat to us?"

"No, sir," Natokah replied. "I don't think so, but it remains an unknown."

"Hmmm," he mused. "Clearly, more information is needed. If the shadowrunners were eliminated, we might never know their true objective. Continue with this mission, Natokah. Observe and gather information. Use your own judgment. If there is a clear and immediate danger to our people, take whatever steps are necessary to neutralize it. Otherwise, simply continue to observe, particularly anything that may involve the Salish-Shidhe."

"Yes, sir," the shaman replied, bowing his head in acknowledgement.

"You have done well," the old man said to him. "Do not needlessly endanger the position you have developed in Seattle. You are far too valuable to us as an active observer in the metroplex."

"I understand, sir," Natokah said.

"We will make arrangements through the usual channels," the old man said. "Do you have anything further to report?"

"No, sir, nothing further."

"Then you are dismissed. Walk in beauty, Natokah," he said.

"Walk in beauty," the shaman replied. He made a deep and respectful bow to his superior, then turned and passed through the walls of the lodge, back into the outside world. The land and sky whirled past as Natokah traveled back to his physical form, straight and true as an arrow. He passed through the walls and wards of his home and settled back into his own skin.

There was a moment of disorientation, the feeling of sudden weight and a slight stiffness from lying on the floor. Natokah breathed deeply, smelling the sweet smoke of the sage, and listened to the beat of the drum. Then he opened his eyes and slowly sat up.

He shut off the music and returned the lights to their normal level, squinting against the sudden brightness. As he put everything back in its proper place, his thoughts focused on the upcoming run. The sooner Draven secured passage across the border to Lewiston, the sooner Natokah could find out what it was in Native American territory that so interested these shadowrunners.

"Murder?"

Midnight nodded. "The authorities in the Sioux Nation say Natokah murdered his brother before he fled the country and landed in Seattle—that was about a year ago. There's still an outstanding warrant for his arrest."

"That's probably why he wanted to know where exactly we were going."

Midnight nodded again. "Probably part of the reason. The Salish-Shidhe Council shares a border with the Sioux, and all the Native American Nations have extradition agreements and treaties. If Natokah is caught in NAN territory, odds are good he'll be shipped home to face charges."

"Why did he kill his brother?"

Midnight shrugged. "The report didn't say. You'd have to ask him—though I don't think I would."

"You think he's a danger to the team?"

"I don't really know," Midnight replied thoughtfully. "Natokah has a solid professional reputation in Seattle, even though he's only been working the shadows for about a year. Everything I've heard says he can be trusted to get the job done. But regardless of how trustworthy he appears, this seemed important enough to bring up.

"Since you asked my opinion," Midnight continued, "I think Natokah is worth having on the team. He knows the NAN territory, and he's experienced in dealing with the Awakened wilderness. He's a capable shaman and he's a pro with a good rep. All that being said, I think we should keep a close eye on him. Just like every other shadowrunner, he's got his own interests, and once we're out of the metroplex, he may decide they're more important than his loyalty to the team. If there's an "accident" and he's the only one who makes it back to Seattle . . ."

Kellan's head jerked up and she stared at Midnight. The elf just shrugged.

"I'm not saying it'll happen," she said, "just that we should be careful. Keep an eye on Natokah, Kellan, and I'll watch your back."

"Right," Kellan nodded. Great. Orion didn't trust Midnight. Midnight didn't trust Natokah. Natokah clearly didn't trust Kellan. And on the eve of leading her own run, Kellan wasn't sure she could trust anyone.

15

The lava flats in Puyallup were known as Hell's Kitchen for good reason. During the Ghost Dance War, Native American shamans awakened dormant Mount Rainier. The volcano erupted, raining ash down over Seattle and covering parts of Puyallup in flows of molten lava. Streams and lakes that filled with ash and were buried under lava fifty years ago had turned into bubbling pools of mud, and geysers that erupted in boiling water from time to time. Everything else in the area was a barren wasteland of igneous rock.

A few corporations began building geothermal energy plants on the lava plains, but the Crash of '29 scuttled those plans. Now Hell's Kitchen was filled with abandoned buildings, some half buried in solidified magma and ash. Only scavengers—human and otherwise—still lived there, picking clean the skeletons of the buildings and scuttling across the lava flats looking for other salvage, risking the unpredictable geysers of steam and treacherous boiling mud.

The same qualities that made Hell's Kitchen a no-man's-land made it perfectly suited for some inhabitants of the metroplex. It was located close to the official borders of Seattle and was difficult to patrol. The Metroplex Guard—UCAS military protection for the city-state of Seattle—relied heavily on automated monitoring stations scattered along the border that served as listening posts for illegal border activity. Such monitors offered a limited level of efficiency, and smugglers quickly found ways to slip past them and move undetected into and out of the Seattle area.

So, on the day after Kellan's meeting with Midnight, she assembled her team of shadowrunners in Hell's Kitchen just past midnight. It was nearly pitch-dark on the lava fields, the only illumination the stars overhead and the lights of the metroplex glittering off to the north and west. This was where they would meet the driver who would take them out of Seattle and into the Native American Nations. Draven had gotten lucky with one of his contacts—the smuggler had a run scheduled in the direction they wanted to go, and the space to accommodate the team.

They stashed their own transportation on the outskirts of Hell's Kitchen in a garage run by the Razor Heads, a local gang willing to keep your ride safe for a fee. They walked the remaining few kilometers out onto the lava flats, guided by Natokah and Orion.

The shaman knew the hazards of the area and the pickup location, and Orion's elven vision allowed him to see his surroundings as easily as if it were daylight. Nobody said much as they walked, but Kellan had a knot of nervous excitement in her stomach. *This was it. The run was a go.* She tried to keep a careful eye on everyone in the team, alert for any signs of trouble from within or from without.

After what seemed like hours, Natokah consulted his handheld global positioning system one final time, then called a halt. The team hunkered down in the darkness and waited. There was little conversation, though Draven muttered a quiet monologue as he checked over his pack and supplies. Orion stuck close by Kellan, apparently convinced that she needed protection. Midnight and Natokah were like silent shadows on the edges of the group, both watching and waiting as a distant roar grew closer.

The smuggler drove a thunderbird, a low-altitude, vector-thrust vehicle perfectly suited for the rough terrain of the lava flats. It roared over the uneven ground, the sinkholes and the mud pools with aplomb. Its running lights stabbed the darkness, showing the profile of something that looked like a flying bus with stubby fins and huge jet engines at the back. Its dorsal surface bristled with sensors and gun turrets, like a tank—which, essentially, it was.

The roar from the engines diminished only slightly as the vehicle slowed, then it came in for a landing on an open swath of the flats, the sound of the thrusters dropping off to a whine, but the engines still kicking up a thick cloud of dust and ash.

"Let's go!" Kellan shouted and signaled the rest of the group, shouldering her pack and loping off toward the t-bird. The other shadowrunners followed suit as a hatch popped open in the side of the vehicle. Natokah reached it first and pulled it fully open. He jumped inside, dropped his pack out of the way and offered his hand to help the others up. Kellan saw the name LEAPIN' LIZARD painted in green letters along the prow of the vehicle.

In short order, they were packed inside the close confines of the LAV's cabin. Natokah slid the hatch closed, and the engines began revving up again. The cabin was surprisingly quiet, the sound of the engines reduced to a dull, muffled roar.

"Mornin', folks." An electronically filtered voice came through the speakers in the cabin. "I'm Fast Eddy, and I'm gonna get you out to Lewiston. Everybody get strapped in, cuz we're gonna be moving fast." Kellan immediately fumbled with the safety harness built into the seat, slipping her arms through the straps and buckling the harness in the middle of her chest. She felt the thunderbird lift off the ground and turn, she assumed, to the southeast.

"Let's ride!" Fast Eddy's voice called over the speakers. Then the thunderbird rocketed forward with a force that slammed Kellan against the seat and, painfully, against Orion's shoulder. They picked up speed, and the roar of the engines increased.

"Things might get a little bumpy back there," the rigger pilot added. "Just hang on and stay frosty. I've run this route plenty of times, so there's nothing to worry about."

Kellan spotted the dim light of an intercom switch on the comm panel near her head. She pressed it, speaking to the empty air. "How long to Lewiston?"

"Couple hours, tops," came the response, "depends on what things are like along the way, but I'm not expecting any problems. Sorry, but there's no in-flight movie. Just so ya don't get too bored back there, I'm gonna set it up so you can watch the HUD."

A heads-up display rotated down from the ceiling of the compartment until it was almost flush against the front wall. It was about half a meter across, and immediately it lit up with a computer-generated view of the terrain—a feed from the thunderbird's sensors. It showed ground contours and other shapes picked up by the LAV's radar and infrared imaging systems. Kellan assumed that, like all riggers, the smuggler was plugged directly into the t-bird's systems, "seeing" and "hearing" everything its sensors picked up.

The shadowrunners remained silent as they watched the screen. The thunderbird flew faster than most ground transportation moved, though it was clear Fast Eddy wasn't going full tilt. The smuggler was tempering the vehicle's capabilities to accommodate the uneven terrain and the darkness, and to reduce the risk of detection. Kellan couldn't judge their velocity by how quickly they passed their surroundings as shown on the heads-up display, but she'd be willing to bet they were going faster than a bullet train. In almost no time, the rigger's voice came over the speakers again.

"We're getting close to the border. We should be across in just a couple of minutes. That's when the fun starts."

Kellan tensed in her seat, watching the display and feeling helpless at her inability to control the situation. The smuggler was a pro, and Draven vouched for Fast Eddy's reputation, so she just had to trust that everything would go well. None of the other runners appeared nervous, though they all focused on the display as the t-bird ate up the kilometers between them and the border of the Seattle Metroplex and the Salish-Shidhe Council.

Suddenly, a small red light flashed on the viewscreen.

"What's that?" Kellan asked aloud.

"Trouble," Draven muttered, just as Fast Eddy announced, "We've got company, folks! Two bogeys headed in. I'm going to try and shake 'em, so hang tight!"

Kellan felt her stomach lurch as Fast Eddy dropped the t-bird's altitude to fly perilously close to the ground in an attempt to confuse any radar or other scan that tried to pinpoint their location. A second window opened up on the display screen, showing an overhead view of the area. Two red blips were closing in on a green dot that represented the *Leap-in' Lizard*.

"They've spotted us!" Fast Eddy said. "We're gonna have to make a run for it."

They picked up more speed, but the red blips continued to close in. Then an alarm beeped from the speakers as a smaller blip detached from one of the bogeys, streaking toward the t-bird.

"Missile!" Draven shouted, just as the thunderbird lurched in an evasive maneuver. A muffled blast shook the cabin, slamming the shadowrunners against their safety harnesses and sending the LAV skidding sideways before it regained its forward momentum.

"That felt close!" Orion said.

"Hang on, we got another one incoming!" Fast Eddy warned. There was another explosion, this one not quite as close as the first, though the vibrations still shook the cabin as the thunderbird zigged and zagged to create the most difficult target possible.

"Can you use magic to take care of them?" Orion asked, and Kellan shook her head.

"I need to see them," she replied. "It has to be a direct line of sight. A video link or tactical display isn't enough." She looked at Natokah, silently asking if the shaman had any tricks up his sleeve.

"I may be able to help," he said, "but not until we clear this terrain." He didn't elaborate any further. He merely closed his eyes and slumped in his seat, a position that Kellan knew meant the shaman was astrally projecting.

The t-bird hugged the terrain, keeping its distance from its pursuers, but it had to swerve to avoid obstacles on the ground—a problem that didn't seem to affect their attackers. Another volley of missiles closed in, missing by a narrow margin and shaking the cabin with the force of their blasts. The overlay map on the display showed the Salish-Shidhe border coming up quickly.

"It's not the UCAS border patrol," Natokah announced, raising his head and opening his eyes. "They're Lone Star assault choppers."

"Lone Star?" Kellan asked. "What the frag are they doing here?"

The shaman shook his head. "I don't know. Border patrol isn't in Lone Star's jurisdiction. They're only supposed to handle law enforcement inside the metroplex."

"Well, somebody should tell them that!" Orion said as another blast shook the t-bird.

"The good news," Midnight interjected, "is that they should break off once we cross the border. Lone Star doesn't have any authority outside the metroplex, and I'll bet they won't want to create an incident with the NAN authorities."

"We'd better hope so," Kellan replied, "but what about the SSC border patrol? They must have noticed all of this drek going on right on their doorstep!"

"I think I can handle that," Natokah said. Kellan was about to ask him how, when Fast Eddy's voice came over the speakers again.

"Border's coming up!" The thunderbird shot across the line on the map separating the Seattle Metroplex from Salish-Shidhe Council territory. The red dots following close behind them slowed.

"I think they're breaking off," Orion said.

"Yeah, but look there." Draven pointed at the upper corner of the screen, where a pair of blue dots appeared.

"Great, more company," Kellan muttered. Could anything else go wrong with the start of their run?

Natokah began chanting in a low, deep tone, calling out over the thrumming of the thunderbird's engines. His chant rose in volume and pitch, and once again Kellan had the impression of a shadowy shape overlaying the shaman's features. His face took on a sharper cast and, as he raised his arms toward the ceiling, Kellan caught a glimpse of mighty wings spreading behind him. With the shaman's final cry, there was a flicker in the air, and Kellan shivered, sensitive to the magic washing over her.

Natokah spoke firmly in a language Kellan didn't know. She assumed it was the shaman's native tongue.

"The intercom," he said to Kellan. She blinked for a second, and then hit the TALK button.

"Eddy," the shaman said, "change course to get clear of our last heading."

"Roger that," the pilot replied.

On the screen, the icon for the t-bird shifted course a bit further south. Within a minute, the red blips of the Lone Star choppers dropped off the screen and the incoming blue blips veered off toward the area of the border where the thunderbird had emerged, but away from the LAV's current position.

"What did you do?" Kellan asked Natokah. The shaman exhaled heavily.

"I called upon the aid of a spirit of the land," he said, "to conceal our presence. We are hidden from the eyes of the border patrol for the time being. By the time they finish investigating why Lone Star has been active so close to the border, we should be long gone."

"You mean we're invisible?" Orion asked, and Natokah shook his head.

"No. More like well camouflaged."

"For how long?" Kellan asked.

"Until sunrise. More than long enough to get us where we're going. I don't think we should have any other trouble with patrols before we reach Lewiston."

Kellan was impressed. She'd never even seen Lothan do something like this.

"Nice work," she told Natokah, and the shaman nodded in acknowledgement.

"What troubles me," he said, "is why Lone Star assault choppers showed up so close to the border."

"Only one reason," Midnight spoke up. "Someone told them to be there."

"What do you mean?" Orion asked.

The security specialist looked at each of the other shadowrunners in the cabin. "I mean someone tipped them off about a border crossing," she said. "Some-

one convinced Lone Star it was in their best interest
to intervene, even outside their normal jurisdiction."

"You mean one of us," Kellan said flatly.

Midnight shrugged. "I mean someone who knew
we were headed out of the Metroplex. Who else is
there aside from us?"

I can think of a few people, Kellan thought. G-Dogg,
Jackie Ozone, Lothan. Would any of them sell her
out to Lone Star? Kellan didn't want to believe that.
Then there was whoever killed Squeak. Maybe they
had an in with the Star? Hell, maybe Lone Star killed
him. The other alternative was what Midnight suggested: one of her team tipped off the corp about
their run. But who, and why?

"We're in the clear for now," Natokah said, cutting
through the strained silence. "We won't have to
worry about Lone Star in Lewiston. They don't have
many contracts in Salish-Shidhe territory."

The shadowrunners watched the display screen as
the *Leapin' Lizard* roared across the countryside of the
Salish-Shidhe Council toward their destination, more
as a way to avoid conversation than out of any real
interest. Kellan knew they were all wondering the
same thing. Was one of them—maybe even more
than one—willing to sell out the rest of the team? If
there was a traitor in their midst, then they had a lot
more to worry about than evading a Lone Star patrol.
A *lot* more.

16

They reached the outskirts of Lewiston with no further incidents, and the Salish-Shidhe patrols ignored them. It took less than two hours to arrive at their destination, just as Fast Eddy promised.

The smuggler chose an isolated spot a couple of kilometers from the town and brought the *Leapin' Lizard* in for a smooth landing. The shadowrunners unbuckled their harnesses and climbed out of the flying tank, grateful to have their feet on solid ground again. The wooded clearing was silent apart from the slowing whine of the t-bird's engines and the pinging noise of heated metal cooling in the night air. Kellan glanced at her chronometer; it was still a couple of hours before dawn.

The forward hatch of the thunderbird hissed open and a lithe figure wearing a dark blue flight suit and a helmet with a dark visor climbed out. The helmet was trailing several cables, which connected to the systems on board the *Lizard;* inputs in the helmet jacked directly into the pilot's neural ports. Fast Eddy reached up and pulled off the helmet, releasing a luxurious length of auburn hair that she shook out as she stowed the helmet in the cockpit.

She jumped down from the LAV and approached Kellan with her hand extended.

"Kellan? Nice to meet you." Kellan shook the proffered hand. The rigger's fingers were tough and calloused. "Draven said you were looking for a round trip?"

Kellan nodded. "Yeah. Can you give us a minute to talk it over?"

"Sure thing. I'm going to do a quick check to make sure ol' *Liz* didn't take any damage from those close volleys." She jerked a thumb over her shoulder toward the t-bird. "Let me know."

As soon as the rigger was out of earshot, Kellan turned to the rest of the team, who were waiting expectantly.

"Okay," she said. "We're headed for a place in Hell's Canyon, not too far from Lewiston."

Natokah nodded. "That's rough terrain. We'll need to take an all-terrain vehicle, or else a boat down the Snake River to get there. I would recommend the river, if it's willing."

"What do you mean 'if it's willing'?" Orion asked. "How do you find out if a river is willing?"

"You ask it," Natokah replied seriously.

"How long to get there, look around and get

back?" Kellan interrupted. The shaman thought for a moment.

"I'd say three, maybe four days."

"Okay," Kellan said. "So if I ask Fast Eddy to pick us up in five days, we should be good."

Kellan waved at Fast Eddy to get her attention. The rigger rejoined them, reporting no significant damage to her thunderbird. She seemed rather pleased about their brush with Lone Star. "Helps liven up the short runs," she explained. Kellan asked the rigger to meet them at this same location in five days, and she nodded in agreement.

"No problem," she said. "I'll be on my way back by then, and I'll make sure there's enough room for you in the back." Kellan paid the rigger for their trip in-country, along with a small retainer for the return. As she made the transaction, her thoughts flickered briefly to Brickman. Could he be setting them up? Was that how Lone Star knew to come for them? There was no love lost between Brickman's Knight Errant employers and Lone Star, but then, that made Lone Star the perfect tools, since no one would suspect Brickman of being involved with them. But how would he know when and from where they were leaving . . . ?

Stop it. You're getting paranoid. Of course, some considered paranoia a survival skill in the shadows. Personally, Kellan considered it a distraction.

Once her business was concluded, Fast Eddy buttoned up inside the *Leapin' Lizard*. She waited until the runners were clear of the area before firing up the t-bird's engines again. The LAV rose up from the clearing to an altitude above the treetops and took off, heading south. Soon it was lost from sight, and even the sound of its turbines faded.

The shadowrunners easily covered the few kilometers to town, and slipped in just before the sun began to rise. Kellan was actually happy to stretch her legs after the hours inside the cabin of the t-bird, though walking through dark woods wouldn't have been her first choice of exercise. Natokah seemed at home tracking through the forest, however, and guided them on an easy path.

Like most cities and towns in the NAN, Lewiston was already old before the United Canadian and American States ceded territory to the Native Americans, and it still looked much as it had around the turn of the twenty-first century. There were some native touches in the style of the newer construction, similar to what she had seen in Natokah's neighborhood of Columbia back in Seattle, but there was little else to distinguish it as part of the NAN.

Kellan decided the first orders of business were food and transportation. She assigned Midnight and Draven the task of scoping out the downtown area and locating a place to eat, and places where they could pick up the supplies they needed. Kellan took Orion and Natokah to look into transportation downriver to Hell's Canyon. She hoped they could accomplish all this without attracting unwanted attention—with any luck, anyone who thought twice about the runners would assume they were campers or tourists.

The boat rental places were open early, and they were able to find one that had a motorized pontoon boat available. Kellan used her Ms. Webley ID to handle the transaction, which would provide cover if they had to ditch the boat. The owner of the establishment, an older man of mixed Native American and Anglo ancestry, was eager to chat, and confirmed that a trip downriver would take at least two days, possibly longer.

"Depends on how far you plan to go," he added. "The Snake River stretches on for quite some distance. You're only going to be able to go so far downriver before you run into some rapids. Boat like this won't go over most rapids." He repeated that point several times as they discussed the security deposit and rules for safe use of the craft. "You can ford across some of the rapids, of course, but that will add time to your trip. Where are you planning on going?"

Kellan considered for a moment, and then described their destination. He shook his head.

"Oh, that's downriver quite a ways, near Granite Creek and the Seven Devils. You'll never go all that way in a boat like this. You need a kayak or something that can handle the rapids. And even then you'd need to ford some of them."

Kellan glanced over at Orion and Natokah. The shaman shook his head slightly and turned to the owner.

"Well, we'll have to change our plans a bit, then," he said. "I told them it would be difficult to go so far downriver in a boat. Maybe we'll leave the river earlier than planned and do some hiking, instead." His expression told Kellan to play along, so she did.

"Yeah, I guess so," she said, trying to sound disappointed, which wasn't too hard. They concluded their business, then the man took them behind his shop and showed them the boat they'd rented. Kellan told him they would be back in a few hours to take possession.

As they made their way back to meet up with the other runners, Kellan turned to Natokah.

"What was all that about? If we can't make it far enough downriver . . ."

"We can," the shaman replied. "But it's simpler if we don't have to explain to anyone *how* we're going to do that." He smiled. "I doubt it's covered by the rental company's insurance policy."

"Magic?"

Natokah nodded. "The rapids will pose no problem, and we will cover the distance faster than predicted."

Kellan didn't ask for any details. Should she? If Natokah was confident they could make it, she guessed she was willing to take him at his word, for the moment.

They met up with the rest of the team, who'd found a local diner open and serving breakfast. There were a few other hardy souls up at the crack of dawn; a couple of hikers, several elderly locals and a handful of truckers—legitimate versions of Fast Eddy—passing through Lewiston on their way elsewhere. Kellan wondered if any of them were really smugglers, perhaps with rigs of their own stashed somewhere outside of town.

They chose a table in the back, well away from the other patrons, and ordered. Kellan noticed that soy did not appear anywhere on the menu. When she pointed that out to the rest of the team, only Natokah seemed pleased at the prospect of eating unprocessed food. Unsure of what any of the food was going to taste like, everyone but Natokah stuck with the somewhat familiar and ordered the special: pancakes, eggs and bacon or sausage, plus coffee.

Once the waitress had poured their coffee and headed off to other tables, Kellan took the opportunity to tell Draven and Midnight about the arrangements for taking a boat to go downriver into Hell's Canyon.

"Natokah says he can get us there faster than normal," she said, glancing over at the shaman. He nodded in response.

"Does it have to be by river?" Draven asked, with a somewhat pained look. "Water and me . . ." He trailed off. The dwarf had taken off his horned helmet and stashed it along with his pack beside the table, but he still looked like a refugee from the set of a fantasy sim. Kellan hoped his distinctive appearance wasn't drawing too much attention—though she had to admit that no one in the diner seemed interested in them.

"What's the matter?" Midnight teased. "Can't swim?"

"I can swim," Draven replied, "it's just that I'm better at sinking."

"Well, you can walk," Kellan said. "But it's a fraggin' long hike."

The dwarf sighed in resignation.

"You will not be able to wear your chain mail in the boat," Natokah observed. Draven sighed again and nodded.

"If things go well," the shaman said, "we can make the trip in less than half the normal time, which will allow us additional time to deal with our objective." He looked pointedly at Kellan, but she wasn't about to discuss their goal in public.

She ignored the implied question. "If we get back early, that makes it look like we haven't gone all that far. We can wait in town until our ride gets back, or we can make alternate arrangements."

"We'll probably need to wait," Orion said. "I'm guessing there aren't a lot of options."

Natokah nodded. "We could camp out for an extra day or two, if necessary," he said in a low voice. "It would be safer than risking drawing attention to ourselves in town."

"Frag that," Orion said. "I'm not gonna spend any longer than I have to out in the woods. Give me a coffin hotel over some flimsy tent any day."

"We'll see," Kellan said firmly. There was no getting away from the fact that she and her team were creatures of the urban environment. She was glad that Natokah was so comfortable in the wilderness, but she wasn't entirely happy about having to rely so heavily on the shaman during this part of the run. Ultimately, she realized, they didn't have much choice; if they were going to complete the run, they needed Natokah's help. Kellan was a little surprised that the shaman hadn't tried to negotiate for a bigger share in the profits, especially once he realized how inexperienced his teammates were in wilderness survival.

Their food arrived, interrupting her train of thought. Kellan cautiously forked a bite of scrambled eggs into her mouth and chewed. The texture was strange, but the taste was fresh and intense. She quickly tried the sausage and pancakes. The difference between the soy products she was used to and the real thing was subtle, but she definitely could get used to the real thing—though she realized she probably couldn't afford it in Seattle. As they ate, they reviewed the supplies and equipment they had carried with them from Seattle.

Everyone had packed a supply of dehydrated food and the personal items Natokah had recommended. They had divided the other wilderness essentials between them—medkit, folding shovels, lightweight thermal blankets, a tiny camp stove, a few pans and a water filtration system. They had decided to buy tents and water packs in Lewiston, and Midnight and Draven had already located the nearest store selling camping equipment. Once everyone finished eating, Kellan paid the bill, then they walked to the neighborhood hardware store—which was surprisingly well supplied—and purchased the tents, water packs and a few other items Natokah deemed useful. Then they returned to the riverside.

Natokah naturally took charge of the boat, assigning everyone places to sit and making sure the gear was properly stowed. Then he fired up the outboard engine and they headed away from the docks, down the winding river. By the time they were underway, the sun was fully above the horizon and the day was looking clear. The air was crisp and pleasantly cool, entirely unlike the constant petrochem stink of the metroplex. Kellan looked around at the thick foliage, amazed that such unspoiled places still existed. In her experience, it seemed like nearly every inch of earth had been paved over for a mini-mall, a coffin hotel and a Stuffer Shack. The wilderness was at once fascinating and alien; it was like another world.

Once they were a good distance from Lewiston, out of sight of the docks and on an uninhabited part of the river, Natokah cut the outboard engine. The boat drifted, carried along by the strong current.

"All right," the shaman said to Kellan. "I think it's time we discussed the purpose of our run." His intent was obvious; if Kellan wasn't forthcoming, then

Natokah had no further reason to continue. Kellan didn't mind his challenge, since she had planned to reveal the final details to the team once they left civilization behind.

"Now's as good a time as any," she agreed. She took a deep breath. "I have information on the location of a secret military cache belonging to the old United States," she said. "It was established before the Ghost Dance War, and abandoned when this territory was relinquished to the Salish-Shidhe. It's not in any official records, and all evidence indicates the Native American Nations don't know it exists."

A slow smile split Draven's bearded face as he realized the potential of the payoff. Midnight and Orion, who already knew the objective, watched the reactions of the other shadowrunners.

Natokah showed no reaction. "What's in this secret military cache?"

Kellan shrugged. "I don't know exactly. I do know that there is strong evidence showing that it was not decommissioned, and no evidence indicating that it has been found."

"So it might not contain anything of value."

"That is a possibility," she admitted, "but I said from the beginning that there was some risk involved in the run. It seems just as likely that it contains a lot of milspec equipment and supplies, just waiting to be found."

"Stuff that's, like, forty, fifty years out of date," Draven commented.

"Still worth a bundle on the shadow market," Orion interjected, shooting Draven a glance that said the weapons cache wasn't the only thing the elf considered might be out of date. "We're talking milspec stuff from the war—definitely enough to turn a profit."

"The information about the site alone could be worth quite a bit to the right buyer," Natokah mused aloud.

"Got somebody in mind?" Midnight asked, and the shaman shrugged.

"Maybe. Let's see what's there first." He turned back to Kellan. "So where is this place, exactly?"

"In the Seven Devils Mountains," Kellan said, pulling out a datapad. She brought up a map. "We should be able to follow Bernard Creek as it branches off the river most of the way to the cache. Then we'll have to hike about five kilometers to the site." She handed the datapad to Natokah, who looked over the map and nodded.

"The datapad has coordinates programmed into a GPS locator," Kellan concluded. "Should lead us right there."

"Passcode protected?" Natokah asked.

"Naturally," Kellan said. *And encrypted.* If Natokah or anyone else got the idea they didn't need Kellan once she'd told them what the run was about, they were sadly mistaken.

Natokah handed the datapad back to Kellan without further comment. "We should be on our way, then."

The shaman sat cross-legged in the boat, closed his eyes and began to sing. The words again were in his native tongue, and the song had a flowing quality. It seemed to match the movement of the waters around them, rising and falling in a hypnotic rhythm. The shadowrunners remained completely quiet as Natokah sang, respecting the magician at his work.

The shaman raised his hands over his head and opened his eyes. The sunlight showed his pupils enlarged, so almost none of the whites of his eyes showed, and they were golden-brown, like the eyes of a predatory bird, rather than their usual black. The song ended with a piercing cry that echoed across the river and into the trees.

There was a moment of profound silence. Even the sound of the river seemed to stop. Then it resumed stronger than before, and a rippling wave caused the boat to bob and bounce. Off to starboard, a swirl of white water appeared, like a miniature whirlpool. Draven grabbed for the safety line on the boat, but Natokah gazed calmly at the river. The waters swirled and bubbled, then burst upward as an enormous figure took shape.

It looked like a giant snake, its body so thick that Kellan felt certain she couldn't get her arms all the way around it. Only a portion of it reared up from the surface of the water, but it towered over the boat.

It had a blunt, triangular head, which looked down at the shadowrunners with flat, dark eyes. A forked tongue flickered to taste the air. The snake's body looked as solid as if it were carved from ice, but they could see water flowing through it as quickly as the river was moving. The surface of the snake was covered with shimmering translucent scales, and it swayed slightly in the air above them.

"Great Snake River," Natokah intoned. "I call upon you to carry us on your back to the place that we seek. Make our journey swift and secure. Watch over us and guard us against all danger. I ask this with respect for you and your domain, noble spirit."

The watery serpent regarded Natokah for a long moment, its alien features unreadable. It did not respond immediately, and Kellan had the strong impression of some unspoken communication passing between shaman and spirit. Perhaps the river spirit was assessing Natokah and his companions to decide if they were worthy. Then its blunt head dove toward the boat.

The river spirit encircled the boat in its coils like a breaking wave, sending a ripple out against the flow of the water. Natokah fired up the outboard engine and shouted, "Hang on!"

An instant later, they shot forward as if propelled out of a cannon. The boat sent up a sheet of water from its prow as it cut through the river at a speed far greater than it could ever achieve on its own. The riverbanks rushed past, and Kellan clung to the safety ropes, in fear for her life. After a few minutes, she realized that despite their great speed, the boat remained stable. After overcoming his initial shock, Orion grinned and let out a wild whoop of excitement, like a kid on a carnival ride.

When they saw the foaming white water in the distance, dark rocks thrusting up from the surface, the shadowrunners tensed. Kellan called out a warning to Natokah in the back of the boat.

"The rapids!" she shouted over the roar of the outboard and the water.

"Just hold on!" he shouted back.

Kellan clutched the safety ropes even tighter and hunkered down as they rushed toward the swirling rapids. Rather than being dashed on the rocks or torn apart, as she expected, their boat seemed to skip blithely across them, light as a feather, buoyed up from below. It was like the river swelled to cover the rapids in order for them to pass. Then they dropped back down to the normal surface level and continued on their way.

They made their way downriver past several more rapids before reaching the mouth of Bernard Creek. The boat slowed and gently slid from the Snake River into the tributary. Their speed dropped to what might be expected from the power of their outboard motor, and they chugged up into the creek.

"Damn!" Orion couldn't stop grinning. "What a ride!"

"We've made good time," Natokah observed laconically, like he did this sort of thing all the time. "I estimate that we should be able to make it to our destination by nightfall. We have cut at least a day off our trip."

"Nice work," Kellan complimented him, and the shaman nodded.

"Let's hope what we're looking for makes it worth it," he replied.

17

After the exhilaration of their trip downriver, piloting the boat along the creek and then hiking through the woods seemed rather anticlimactic. If they reached the target site before nightfall, as Natokah predicted, and things went well, they'd be able to head back the following morning with information to sell in Seattle, and hopefully some samples of the abandoned materiel to go with it.

Kellan thought about what she would do with her share of a score. It gave her something to do besides think about how her feet ached in her boots or how her pack seemed to get heavier and heavier the farther they went. She would definitely move into a more upscale place, maybe something in Queen Anne or Capitol Hill. She could invest some cred into magical gear, too, instead of borrowing Lothan's stuff. Her own magical library, maybe, along with some ritual tools, maybe even a place where she

could create a summoning circle. She imagined showing that off to Lothan and seeing what he thought of
her skills then.

Of course, she would spend some on nice clothes,
and a night out on the town from time to time. She'd
heard the Eye of the Needle was one of the nicest
restaurants in Seattle. It was hard to get reservations,
but money talked. She imagined walking into one of
Seattle's most exclusive nightspots, with the shadows
abuzz about what she'd accomplished. "There goes
Kellan Colt," they would say. "Did you hear about
the job she pulled off?"

"Kellan? Kellan?"

"Huh?" Kellan was suddenly yanked out of her
fantasy by Orion's voice. The elf stood close at hand,
adjusting the straps of his pack over his jacket, a
sheen of sweat on his forehead.

"Natokah says we should be pretty close."

Kellan noticed that Draven was lagging a bit behind the rest of the group, while Natokah was a little
ahead, followed closely by Midnight. The two of
them made good time, while the dwarf was ham-
pered by his inexperience in tramping through the
wilderness and by the amount of equipment he
was carrying.

Kellan pulled out the datapad and checked the
global positioning system.

"He's right," she said. "We're pretty close to the
coordinates. It shouldn't be too much farther." Good
thing, too, since she could see the sun sinking toward

the horizon, and the shadows were getting increasingly long, especially under the canopy of the trees towering above them.

Draven came puffing and wheezing up the slope.

"We'd fraggin' better be almost there," the dwarf grunted. "I'm too damn old for this drek."

Ahead was a low rise, and Natokah waved to the rest of the team from there. Midnight waited with him until everyone else caught up.

Below the rise they could see traces of what looked like an old logging road. Only the faint, regularly spaced indentations, overgrown with grasses and ground-covering plants, gave any indication that humans had ever disturbed this place.

"I think this is the way," Natokah said, and Kellan consulted the GPS again.

"It would take us in the right direction," she replied.

"Nobody has been this way for a long time," the shaman observed.

"That's a good sign, right? Means nobody else has found the place yet."

Natokah grunted his agreement.

"You don't sound too happy about it," Kellan said, and the shaman gave her a considering look.

"No, it is promising," he said. "There's just something . . . I don't know, something . . . unsettling about this place."

Perhaps she also was feeling what Natokah had noticed, or maybe it was simply that Kellan was disturbed by the idea that something was making the normally stoic shaman uneasy. She suddenly felt anxious.

A low, throaty growl sounded from the trees to their left. The shadowrunners whipped around toward the sound just as a whirlwind of gray fur exploded from the shadows. It slammed into Natokah, and the shaman and his attacker went tumbling down the slope. Natokah yelled in pain and surprise, and the other shadowrunners sprang into action.

Orion drew his sword and leapt down the slope in a single motion. He tumbled in midair to land lightly on his feet close to where the creature had Natokah pinned to the ground. It was massive, as long as the shaman was tall, and it definitely outweighed him. The beast was all powerful muscle, with a blunt muzzle filled with sharp teeth, and heavy slashing talons on all four paws. Orion attacked and left a bloody gash along its flank, drawing its attention away from Natokah. The beast turned with a fierce growl, jaws flecked with white foam and red blood.

Draven followed close behind Orion, drawing his axe and skittering down the slope, sending loose earth and gravel cascading down ahead of him. The creature's attention remained focused on Orion.

Without moving from her position, Midnight drew her slim pistol and leveled it at the creature, the beam of its laser sight gleaming red in the dying light.

"No!" Kellan said. "You might hit one of the others!"

Midnight flashed her a glance that said she didn't make mistakes like that, then she refocused on the red dot from the laser sight, bringing it to rest on the creature's left shoulder. She pulled the trigger just as it lunged at Orion.

The silenced shot was barely audible above the creature's growls, but a fine spray of blood spurted from where the bullet struck it in the midsection and the animal recoiled, twisting toward this new source of pain. Orion used the opportunity to roll out of the way and come at it from the far side, opposite where Draven was ready to rush it.

The beast's wounds only seemed to enrage it. It howled, and charged at the shadowrunners with renewed fury. Draven swung his axe, but the creature knocked the dwarf aside, sending him flying a good couple of meters. Then Orion dodged in and stabbed, earning another cry of pain from the beast.

From where she stood atop the rise, Kellan concentrated, blocking out the melee below to focus on the maddened creature in its midst. She gathered power to her, shaping it with the force of her will, in the form she'd learned, infusing it with her intent. Draven clambered back to his feet to rush the beast again as it slashed and snapped at Orion. He was barely holding it at bay.

The energy tingled along Kellan's skin until she was like a dam, holding back the power. When it reached the peak of its strength, she pointed at the creature and released the power, letting it leap from her like a bolt of lightning from a cloud to the ground. There was a flicker, barely visible in the mundane world, as the spell struck.

The animal jerked and thrashed as if electrocuted, as the destructive magical power tore into the very fabric of its being. It howled in pain and rage, then hurled itself at Orion, who tried to get out of the way, but was borne down by the creature's furry bulk. The animal thrashed one more time, then lay still.

"Orion!" Kellan yelled. She slid down the slope as quickly as possible, nearly falling as she knocked loose dirt and rocks getting to the old road below. Draven rushed to help the fallen elf. He grabbed the now-limp beast and rolled it off Orion just as Kellan reached them. The hilt of Orion's sword stuck out of the creature's chest, most of the blade buried inside it.

Orion coughed and sputtered and sat up. He was covered with blood, wetly gleaming reddish-black in the shadows. He saw the concern on Kellan's face.

"I'm all right," he said. "I'm all right. It's not my blood. I'm not hurt. What about Natokah?"

Kellan turned to the fallen shaman as Midnight came down the slope and reached his side. Draven helped Orion to his feet, and the elf warrior went to pull his sword from the dead body.

"What the frag is this thing?" Orion asked.

"Greater wolverine," Draven said curtly. "Nasty bastards."

"No drek," Orion said, yanking his sword loose.

Kellan knelt at Natokah's side. There was a ragged tear in his jeans, soaked with blood and revealing an ugly wound. Three bloody slashes stretched from his shoulder down his chest, torn right through his heavy coat. Natokah's head was tipped back, his eyes only slightly open.

Midnight knelt by the shaman's head. "He's in shock," she pronounced, unslinging her pack and opening it, "and still losing blood. Do you know any healing spells?" she asked Kellan. Kellan mutely shook her head.

"We'll have to do this the old-fashioned way, then." Midnight opened up the medkit and took out a trauma-patch. Holding the wrapper in her teeth, she ripped open the package and pressed the adhesive patch against the side of the shaman's neck, the quickest place for the drugs to enter his system.

"Get his coat off," Midnight ordered Kellan. "Make sure there aren't any more of those things out there," she instructed Orion and Draven. Orion wiped his sword on the dead wolverine's fur, but didn't sheath it as he and Draven moved out to secure the perimeter.

Kellan finished working Natokah out of his coat, trying her best to not do any more damage. The slashes along his shoulder and chest were shallow cuts—his armor had blunted that attack. The bite on his thigh was bad. As Kellan eased him back on to the ground, Natokah moaned and stirred.

"Easy, easy," Kellan said, "try not to move."

His breath hissed out from between clenched teeth. "How bad is it?"

"You'll live," Midnight said, "but you probably won't be walking for a while."

"Well, I'll just make myself comfortable here, then."

"We won't leave you," Kellan said.

"You won't have to. Help me sit up."

Kellan slid her hands under Natokah's shoulders and supported him into a sitting position. She felt him wince, but he didn't complain.

"My bag," he said, and Kellan retrieved the fringed leather bag that had fallen nearby when Natokah tumbled down the slope. She held it open, and the shaman withdrew a smaller pouch filled with fragrant dried herbs. With sweat beading on his forehead and streaking the dirt and blood, he took out a small handful and clutched them in his closed fist. Then he began to sing.

It was different from the song he used to raise the river spirit. It was a quiet, soothing song that reminded Kellan of a lullaby. Continuing to sing, Natokah opened the hand holding the herbs and placed it flat against the wound on his leg. He inhaled sharply through clenched teeth and his muscles tensed, then relaxed. Kellan felt a familiar tingle of magic. She opened herself to the astral plane and watched as light spread out from Natokah's hand, extending across and merging with his aura. The places where his aura flickered and went dim grew bright again as the light washed over them.

In a moment, the shaman removed his hand and sat up straight. Looking over his shoulder, Kellan could see the wound in his leg was almost healed. Through the bloody tear in his jeans showed only a moist pink line and some dried blood. The cuts on his chest were completely gone, replaced by smooth, unbroken skin.

With some difficulty, the shaman got to his feet, Midnight and Kellan taking his elbows as he swayed.

"Thanks," he said.

"No problem. I think you should rest a while, though."

"I won't argue with that," Natokah replied, leaning against a nearby tree. It was clear the healing spell had taken considerable effort.

Draven came trotting up the logging road. "This area's clear," he announced.

"Where's Orion?" Kellan looked around for the elf. A moment later, he appeared farther up the road and waved his teammates toward him.

"Hey! Check this out!" he called. Kellan looked a question at Natokah, who nodded.

"I'll be fine," he said. "Let's go."

Orion led them to a wide, flat clearing on the other side of the rise. "Look here," he said, climbing a couple of steps onto a recent spill of dirt and rock.

"There are some metal fragments mixed in with the rock. If we're close to the coordinates for the cache, then I think the entrance to the place might be right around here."

Kellan consulted the GPS locator. "Orion's right," she said. "We're practically on top of it."

"It looks like the military buried it after all," Midnight said, looking around. "If they mined the entire installation, there might not be anything left to find."

"There's only one way to find out." Draven hefted his axe. "We've got to get inside."

"There's no way we're doing that with anything smaller than a backhoe," Orion said. "Our camp shovels won't make a dent against all this." He took in the slope with a sweep of his arm.

Kellan considered the rubble and thought about Lothan's lessons in summoning. She took a deep breath and, before she lost her courage, said, "I can get us in."

"Yeah?" Orion asked.

"Yeah. But it'll take time."

The runners settled into the clearing to wait. Orion and Draven kept a watchful eye out for any other critters that might be lurking in the woods. Orion carefully cleaned his sword, and Draven his axe. Natokah sat cross-legged on the ground, meditating as the last rays of sunlight faded from the clearing.

Kellan spent a few minutes searching through the files on her datapad to find the ritual for what she intended to do. After reading carefully through the information several times, she walked slowly around the clearing, looking for the best area in which to form the ritual circle. When she had chosen the area where she wanted to work, she returned to the pile of rubble and began choosing the rocks she would use to create the patterns and symbols she needed. It took more than an hour to collect enough stones. She started creating the pattern by placing the few crystals she carried at cardinal points around the circle, then used rocks to complete the circle, which was two meters in diameter—the smallest circle she could manage with the materials she was using. Next, she began creating the interior patterns, frequently consulting her datapad to make sure she was getting them right. As she worked, she muttered the words of the ritual over and over, practicing the cadence and tone recommended in the description. Finally, Kellan stood, dusted off her hands on her pants and admired the result of her work.

Busy working on the circle, Kellan didn't notice Midnight had disappeared until she glanced around the clearing and saw no sign of her. Then the elf emerged from around the bend in the road and gestured for Kellan to join her.

"What is it?"

"Come take a look at this." Midnight led Kellan back to where the dead wolverine lay. "I thought we should consider getting rid of this," she said, gesturing toward the corpse with her flashlight, "since it might start attracting the local scavengers once it got dark. When I looked it over, I noticed the condition it was in. Take a look. Notice anything unusual?"

Kellan hunkered down next to the dead body. Although she'd never seen a greater wolverine before (or a lesser one, for that matter) she *did* notice something.

"Its fur is all patchy," she observed. "And those scabs . . ." There were large places on the creature's hide where the hair had sloughed off, leaving red welts and scabs behind.

"I think it was diseased," Midnight said. "That might be why it attacked us."

"Or it just thought we looked like dinner."

"Or maybe it was infected with something, or poisoned by something."

"Poison?" Kellan paused, thinking about it for a minute, then glanced up at Midnight. "Like, from being around chemical weapons?"

Midnight shrugged. "I don't know. But we should be careful. If stuff is leaking into the environment around here, we might be up against more than we bargained for. And Natokah didn't clean out his wounds before he healed them, either."

"Frag. That might be a problem," Kellan said. "I'll tell him."

Natokah listened carefully to Kellan's description of the wolverine's condition and her concerns about the effects of its bite. "My healing magic will protect me from infection," he said confidently, "but it is worrisome that the creature was so ill."

"I'm concerned that it might have been affected by something in the weapons cache," Kellan persisted.

"That is a possibility," he agreed. "We should wear breather masks when we open this up."

Kellan nodded.

Everything was ready. Kellan stepped carefully to the center of the ritual circle. She compared the diagram to the reference in her datapad one last time, just to make sure everything was where it was supposed to be. She thumbed the display to the words of the ritual, just in case she lost her place as she chanted. She took a deep breath, blew it slowly out, and thought to herself, *Well, here goes.*

The chants were slow and sonorous, different from the ones Lothan had used in his demonstration. The intonation rose and fell, and Kellan drifted into a light trance. She focused on the strength and firmness of the earth beneath her feet, and on the ebb and flow of astral energies all around her. As she chanted, she realized Natokah was right—there was something unsettling about the mana in this place. She tried to ignore her feeling of unease and concentrate on the ritual.

She scattered dust to the north, south, east and west. She chanted names of power and stamped her foot on the ground, as if to wake it from a deep slumber. She gathered the mana slowly, painstakingly, molding it to her will and her need. Sweat rolled down her nose and chin. She ignored it, chanting the words, focusing on the earth, shaping the power. Then she spoke the final words of the ritual.

"By the power of air, by the power of fire, by the waters of the deep, and the depths of the earth, I conjure and charge you, arise! Arise and truly do my will! For as I will, so it shall be!"

With those words, Kellan stamped her foot one last time, and a faint tremor seemed to shake the ground. The rich earth in front of her, just outside the circle, rippled and bulged upward. Tearing free of roots and trailing plants, a troll-like figure rose, made of rocky soil. At its full height, it towered over Kellan. Its head was blunt and squared, like a rough-hewn statue, its eyes pools of unfathomable shadow.

"What is your wish?" it asked in a voice like grinding gravel.

Kellan took a deep breath to steady herself. She felt like she'd been running for hours. She pointed to the slope covering the entrance to the weapons cache. "Clear away the obstacles in our path," she said in a firm voice. The earthen figure regarded her for a moment, then bowed its head.

"As you command," the elemental replied, and then it turned toward the slope and bent to its appointed task. The shadowrunners watched in silence. Like a living digging machine, it shoved aside dirt and rock, revealing larger chunks of twisted and charred metal in the rubble. In a matter of minutes, the spirit stepped away from a dark opening into the earth, edged with broken concrete and twisted metal. It turned back to Kellan.

"My task is complete," it announced. When Kellan nodded her agreement, the elemental seemed to sigh and its earthen body suddenly collapsed, becoming an inert pile of rock and soil once more. The spirit animating it returned to wherever it called home. Kellan felt a huge adrenaline rush from successfully summoning the earth elemental. She grinned broadly at her team.

"All right. We're in."

18

Reminding the others to put on their breather masks, Kellan pulled hers out of her pack and started toward the dark opening. Midnight stopped her with a hand on her arm.

"Let me go first."

Kellan thought about insisting on being first, but then acknowledged that Midnight's expertise in getting into—and out of—places was the reason she invited her along in the first place. Kellan followed close behind, along with the other shadowrunners, who had their weapons at the ready. Orion held his sword in his right hand, a pistol in his left. Kellan drew her weapon as well, and carried a flashlight with her free hand.

Inside the opening was a concrete bunker. Kellan saw cracks and burn marks along the entrance. "Looks like they set off explosives to bury the entrance."

"Fortunately, they didn't do a very good job of it," Midnight replied from up ahead. "Either they didn't have the time to destroy the entire place, or they didn't want to risk damaging whatever was inside."

"Maybe they planned to come back," Orion said. "I've always been told that the UCAS assumed they would figure out the magic behind the Ghost Dance eventually."

"That never happened," Natokah replied with a note of pride in his voice.

The space immediately past the entrance was a square, concrete-lined tunnel that extended farther into the earth. Kellan played her light along the ceiling, showing lighting panels mounted in the corners, their fixtures shattered by the blast that buried the entrance.

"Hold it a second," Midnight called back, and the team stopped where they were. Kellan could hear her breath rasping inside her filter mask. Nobody said a word as they stood there.

"All right, it's clear."

They stepped forward so that the beam from Kellan's flashlight reached to where Midnight stood, in front of a doorway that was about two meters wide and three meters tall, covered by a heavy folding door of steel locked across the passage. Midnight was examining the flatscreen console embedded in the wall beside the door.

"Useless," she pronounced. "There's no power. On the good side, that means no alarms, but it also means no way to operate the security system or the door mechanisms."

Draven stowed his weapon and interlaced his fingers, cracking his knuckles. "We'll just have to do it the old-fashioned way, then." Crouching down in front of the door, he grabbed its bottom edge and heaved upward with all his might. The door didn't budge. Draven tried again, muscles bulging, grunting from the effort, but still nothing.

"Not a chance," Midnight said. "That door is locked down tight. You're not getting it open that way."

"What about using magic?" Orion suggested. Before Kellan could answer, Midnight did.

"Not a good idea, unless you know exactly the right spell. There's a better way—which doesn't involve as much effort, either." The elf set down her pack and dug into an interior pocket. In a moment, she came up with what looked like a large tube of toothpaste. She unscrewed the cap and began squeezing a steady line of a sticky white paste on the door. She applied the substance a hand's width from the edge of the door, tracing an unbroken line about a meter and a half long and just over two meters high.

"Thermite paste," she explained, stepping back from the door. She took a small lighter from a pocket of her vest and ignited one end of the white paste. It caught with a faint sputter of sparks and began to slowly burn with an intense heat. Where the paste burned, it cut neatly through the metal. It took several minutes for the thermite paste to burn entirely around the shape Midnight had created, during which time she pressed a small suction cup with a handle to the upper part of the cut-out section, locking it in place with a twist. As the thermite burned out, she nodded to the dwarf.

"Draven?"

Taking hold of the handle, he lifted the cut-out section free from the door.

"Be careful of the edges," Midnight warned him. "They're still hot."

Draven set the section of the door aside and Kellan shined her flashlight beam past him into the space beyond.

It was a good-sized room, at least ten meters across, walled in concrete, with a flat ceiling some three meters above. Much of the room was bare, its floor spotted with dark stains and covered with scattered rubble and discarded packing material. Against the far wall were a number of metal canisters, stacked onto metal racks and covered with a thin layer of dust.

"That's it?" Orion said, looking into the room. "What is this stuff?"

Kellan was disappointed as well. She hadn't been sure what to expect, but from this perspective it looked like the facility *had* been cleaned out before it was abandoned.

"Let's have a look," Midnight said, stepping into the room. Kellan and the others stepped through as well, glancing around warily. As Midnight approached the canisters, Orion cocked his head, like he was trying to identify a distant sound. He said urgently, "Get out of the doorway," waving Draven and Natokah toward the side of the room as they stepped through the entrance. He caught Kellan's arm and gently pushed her toward the wall.

"What is it?" she whispered, but before Orion could reply, she heard it.

Mournful chanting echoed down the passage, steadily growing louder. Midnight stepped away from the metal canisters, and just in time.

As if in response to the chanting, the dark stains on the floor seemed to shiver, become fluid, and then they began to move. They slithered toward each other, picking up each bit of garbage and rubble they touched. Then they swirled into a dark mass that flowed up over the canister closest to the floor. The metal hissed and popped where the liquid touched it until there was a loud *crack*, and a viscous yellow-green ooze poured out of the broken canister, becoming part of the dark mass surrounding it.

"No . . ." Natokah gasped, as the bubbling goo rose, swelling in size. It flowed over another canister, which split open, adding more liquid to the mass. Acrid gas filled the air as the mass began to assume a distinct shape. "We have to get out of here!"

"I'll clear the exit," Orion volunteered. He flattened against the wall as the liquid stretched up toward the ceiling like a pillar, then split down the middle. Kellan had an impression of eyes swirling in the mass.

Orion spun into the doorway, weapons at the ready. As he stepped through, he collided with a shimmering wall that sprang into existence across the opening. There was a greenish flare of light where he came in contact with the wall, and he stumbled back.

"What the frag?" Then he saw the shadowy shape standing on the other side of the mystic barrier. "We've got company."

"Stay out of sight!" Kellan shouted.

"Don't worry," said a muted voice from outside the barrier. "I already have what I want."

"Who the frag are you?" Kellan demanded.

"I'm Zhade," the voice replied. "And I owe you a big thanks. You made finding this place and getting inside really easy."

"You've been following us?"

"Not really," Zhade said. "Let's just say we've been on parallel paths. I just had the advantage of knowing when you would be here."

The mass of fluid and debris shaped itself into two vaguely humanoid forms, each with two arms ending in three fingers, and a head with a recognizable mouth and eyes. They had no legs; they were just swirling pillars of fluid below the arms. They swayed there, eyeing the shadowrunners, who did their best to keep their distance, weapons held at the ready.

"You killed Squeak," Kellan accused Zhade. At that moment, she very much wanted to see her opponent's face. Heedless of her own warning, she stepped out into the room so she could see the entrance.

The shadowy figure stood there, faintly illuminated by the light from the barrier. Zhade was less than a meter from the entrance. He was dressed in mismatched leathers, all straps and buckles, with pieces of what looked like scratched and dirty plastic armor and a tattered plastic slicker worn over it all.

"Who?" he asked, cocking his head.

"Squeak," Kellan repeated. "The guy who found the data on this place."

"Oh, yes, him," Zhade said. "I didn't need to kill him. Someone already had. I assumed it was you. So did the Brain Eaters, apparently."

"Yeah, right," Kellan replied.

Zhade shrugged. "I have no reason to lie to you. In fact, I have no real reason to continue talking to you." He made a broad gesture toward the creatures at the back of the room, as if he were gathering them to him.

With a squishing, sloshing noise, each one bent down and retrieved two of the metal canisters. Then they flowed—first one, then the other—toward the glowing barrier.

Orion raised his pistol, but Natokah called out, "Don't! It won't have any effect, and you might hit one of the canisters."

"Excellent advice," Zhade sneered. The toxic spirits reached the magical barrier and passed through it as if it weren't there. Zhade stepped forward and took the canisters, cradling them gently in his arms as if they were children. Then the toxic creatures withdrew into the chamber with the shadowrunners.

Kellan concentrated, gathering power. There was a foul "taste" to the mystic energies, as if the poisons in the air and the chemicals soaked into the concrete had tainted everything around them. She poured her will against Zhade's barrier and flung a manabolt spell at it. The barrier shimmered and rippled, but it held, and Zhade smiled wickedly.

"Impressive," he said. "Given time, you *might* manage to break through. Too bad you won't have it. Good-bye."

The shaman took a step back from the barrier and spoke an ugly-sounding phrase. Clouds of noxious green mist hissed out from around Zhade's booted feet as he walked slowly backward. Where the fumes touched the walls and ceiling, they began to eat away at the concrete and steel reinforcements.

"They're yours. Don't make them suffer too long," Zhade called out. Then the ceiling gave way outside the mystic barrier, and concrete, rock and dirt buried the entrance with a dull roar. A moment later, the barrier flickered out, leaving the shadowrunners' flashlights and the sickly glow of the toxic spirits as the only source of light in the room.

"Kellan, the spirits," Natokah said, "we have to banish them! We have to—"

The first spirit lashed out at Natokah, and he

ducked as it left chemical scars along the wall where he had stood an instant before.

Orion and Draven leapt toward the other spirit, slashing with sword and axe. Draven struck twice, then backed away with an oath as the blade of his axe began to dissolve. Orion's enchanted blade, on the other hand, carved chunks out of the spirit's shape. Inert fluids splashed to the floor as the spirit thrashed and wailed in pain.

Natokah stood his ground near the wall, facing the other spirit. He spread his hands, traced a warding gesture in the air, and began to sing. The toxic spirit stopped in its tracks, as if an invisible barrier had sprung up between it and its prey. It struggled to reach Natokah, fought against the power of the shaman's will. Though the song wasn't familiar, Kellan knew Natokah was attempting to banish the spirit, forcing it away from the material plane, the mundane part of the world.

Draven cried out as the second spirit's arm flowed across his left shoulder, burning wherever it touched. He managed to break free from its grip when Orion slashed through the arm holding the dwarf. The spirit sprouted another limb from the fluid mass of its body as Draven reeled back. Kellan could see burns seared across his chest and arms, his armor partially melted.

The spirit focused its attention on Orion as the elf warrior danced around it, dodging in to strike with slashes of his gleaming sword, then leaping and dodging out of the way of the spirit's return attacks. Draven charged in with his half-melted axe to strike the spirit again. It batted the dwarf away with one tentacle-like limb. Draven crashed into the wall, losing his helmet and falling in a heap.

Kellan cast a manabolt at the spirit fighting Orion, but the presence of the toxic spirits was contaminating the mana. Her spell was weak and had little effect, and the spirit remained focused on Orion. The elf ducked and rolled to avoid another noxious strike, counterattacking as he regained his feet. This time when he slashed, his blade stuck in the creature's body and was torn from his hands.

The spirit lashed out, striking Orion in the shoulder. There was a sickening hissing sound and the elf stumbled back. He lost his footing on the slick floor and fell. The spirit towered above him, as if it intended to wash over the elf like a wave of burning acid.

"No!" Kellan shouted. Suddenly, everything Lothan had taught her about banishing spirits crystallized in her mind. She focused her will on the spirit, held out her hands and pronounced the ritual of banishment.

The toxic spirit stopped in midlunge, and Kellan felt the force of its malevolent will turn upon her. At that moment, she became fully, sickeningly aware of just how conscious, how deeply twisted, these creatures were. A wave of pure hatred for all living things, a burning desire to corrupt, to destroy threatened to overwhelm her. She steeled her will, and repeated the ritual of banishment.

As if from a distance, she heard Natokah's song as the shaman struggled to do the same. Her words of power mixed with the shaman's song as Kellan exhorted the spirit to be gone and trouble the world no more. It burbled and hissed, thrashing against her will, single-minded in its desire to destroy. Sweat poured down Kellan's face beneath her protective mask. Her breath came in ragged gasps.

With a desperate surge of effort, Kellan pressed the attack and felt the spirit's resistance crumble. The toxic mass abruptly collapsed in on itself, subsiding into a puddle of noxious ooze. The last shrieks of the spirit died away in Kellan's mind as its connection with the physical world was broken and it fled into the depths of the astral plane.

She saw that Orion had struggled to his feet. As the spirit collapsed, he seized the hilt of his sword and pulled it free. Then he turned on the spirit battling Natokah. The shaman fought valiantly, but he was down on one knee, arms raised to ward off the thing towering above him, which was struggling to surge forward and engulf him in its fetid mass.

Orion's sword flashed, once, twice, three times in the blue-white light of the flashlights lying on the floor. The toxic spirit thrashed and twitched as Orion cut apart its body while Natokah leashed its will. It collapsed with a slosh into an inert heap of sludge and refuse.

Natokah started to get to his feet, then his eyes rolled back into his head and he pitched forward, slamming into the floor. Midnight was at his side before Kellan could reach him, pressing slim fingers against the side of the shaman's neck.

"He's alive."

The spirits were gone. Orion looked at the rubble choking the only exit from the bunker and turned to Kellan.

"Can you can recall that elemental?"

Kellan shook her head. "I was only able to bind it for one service."

"Then we're trapped, and as good as dead."

19

"Like fraggin' hell," Kellan declared. She stepped into the middle of the room, away from Natokah's unconscious figure, and faced the entrance, fists clenched at her side, eyes narrowed in anger and concentration. Dammit, it *wasn't* going to end like this! She felt magical power building all around her, hot on her skin.

"Kellan, what are—?" Orion began, but Midnight hushed him.

Kellan was barely aware of her fellow shadowrunners. She called to mind one of Lothan's first lessons, in which he had taught her how to levitate objects. She'd started with small things—her phone, a book—and progressed to larger ones. Still, she'd never moved anything heavier than Lothan himself, and the rubble probably weighed tons. But Kellan didn't think of that. All she was thinking about was how she was responsible for this mess. She was the leader of this team, and she wasn't going to give up without a fight!

Her temperature spiked as magical energy surged around her. The amulet at her throat felt suddenly hot and heavy against her skin. Kellan hurled her will against the debris blocking the entrance.

For a moment there was nothing, just the labored sound of Kellan's breathing. Then some dust and pebbles shook loose from the rubble, pattering to the floor. Kellan gritted her teeth. *Come on, come on!* she thought, pressing with all her will. Orion's words echoed in her head: *We're as good as dead.*

"Come on," she muttered. She was drenched in sweat. It felt like her amulet was burning her skin, but she used the pain to focus her concentration until everything narrowed down to the pile of ferrocrete and metal in front of her.

Kellan threw up her arms and yelled, *"Move!"* and an invisible force suddenly blasted the rubble clear of the entrance, shoving it aside like a bulldozer. A fresh cascade of dirt and dust poured down, but a gap had opened, big enough for them to climb through.

Gasping for breath, Kellan staggered back, clutching her temples against the splitting headache stabbing her brain. Orion grabbed her around the waist with one arm and steadied her against his uninjured shoulder. The elf looked at the passage blasted through the rubble and then down at Kellan.

"Damn," was all he said, clearly impressed.

Kellan, Orion and Midnight somehow managed to haul Draven and Natokah out of the underground chamber and back to the clearing outside. Zhade was long gone. Midnight pulled off her breather mask as soon as they set their unconscious teammates on the ground outside and flipped open her pack. She handed Orion and Kellan a couple of slap-patches each.

"Put these on," she said, "and one onto each of them," nodding toward the others. "They're broad-spectrum antitoxins." They immediately tore open the packaging and applied the patches, while Midnight assessed the team's injuries with a portable medkit.

After she applied the patch to Natokah's neck, Kellan turned to Orion.

"Your shoulder," she said, reaching out but then pulling back, not daring to touch it. Part of the elf's jacket was literally melted away, and his exposed flesh was covered with a blistering burn.

"It's all right," he said quietly. "I'll be okay." But he kept his teeth clenched. She knew it must hurt like hell.

"We're lucky," Midnight pronounced, continuing to study the medkit readout.

"Lucky?" Kellan said incredulously.

"Yes, lucky no one's dead," Midnight replied, "and nobody looks to be fatally injured, either."

"What about Natokah?"

"Mostly exhaustion, I think." Midnight brushed a stray strand of black hair back from her face and wiped sweat from her forehead with the back of her hand. "He used a lot of magic in a short period of time. He's worn himself out. He might have internal injuries, but I can't tell with this equipment."

"Kellan?" Orion turned to her. "What do we do?"

Kellan just stared for a moment, looking from Orion to Midnight and back. After all that had happened, he was still looking to her for direction, for her to take charge.

"I—I don't know," she said, glancing down. She looked at the shadowrunners who almost didn't survive her leadership, who still might not, if they didn't find a way out of Hell's Canyon. It was hours still until sunrise. Who knew what other Awakened predators might be out there in the wilderness? Who knew if Zhade left behind any other surprises for them?

She looked back up at her teammates: Orion looking hopeful and a bit lost, Midnight as composed and calm as ever, patiently waiting for Kellan's answer. She swallowed her fear and doubt. There wasn't time for it right now.

"Can we move them?" she asked Midnight, indicating Draven and Natokah with a nod.

"I think I can bring Draven around," Midnight said briskly, moving over to the dwarf. She applied a stim-patch to the side of Draven's neck, over the artery. In fairly short order, the dwarf regained consciousness with a groan.

"Don't try to move yet," Midnight said. "You've got some burns . . ."

"No fraggin' kidding," the dwarf grumbled through gritted teeth. "Hurts like hell."

"I can give you some beta-endorphins for the pain," Midnight said, picking up the medkit. Draven's hands felt around on the ground next to him.

"My axe?"

"It got melted," Kellan said.

Draven closed his eyes and sighed. "Ah, they just don't make 'em like that anymore." Midnight applied a painkiller near the edge of the burn, and the tense lines in the dwarf's face soon eased.

"We should move to the edge of the clearing and get some rest," Midnight suggested. "Draven's in no shape to travel right now and I don't want to risk bringing Natokah around. We can set a watch, and let them rest as much as possible. We can take stock of things in the morning."

"What about Zhade?" Kellan asked.

"What about him?" Midnight replied. "We've got to worry about ourselves right now. This run is a wash, Kellan. Zhade took or destroyed whatever was left here. We need to cut our losses and worry about getting back to civilization in one piece, and then making it back to the metroplex."

Kellan opened her mouth to object, then closed it. She was so tired, and she felt unsteady on her feet. "You're right. Let's stay here for tonight and see how things look in the morning."

As Midnight cleaned and dressed Draven's wounds and made Natokah comfortable, Kellan and

Orion organized what little there was to their camp. Kellan volunteered to try building a fire, but Midnight recommended against it. So the shadowrunners used their thermal foil blankets to keep warm and ate their dried food in silence in the dark.

Dark and cold suited Kellan's mood. Midnight was right: they were lucky nobody was killed. They were damn lucky they weren't *all* dead. Zhade's spirits would have finished them off if Natokah hadn't helped her banish them. The only thing she gave herself credit for was getting them out of the bunker—and even now, they still might not survive.

She wondered about Zhade. How had he found out about this place? He knew who Squeak was, but claimed he didn't kill him. Why bother lying to someone you're planning to kill? Zhade had nothing to lose by confessing to the warez dood's murder, yet he didn't. Was he working for someone else? And for that matter, what was in the canisters he took?

Eventually, worn down by questions that had no answers, and by the drain of her magic use, Kellan fell into a fitful and dreamless sleep.

Kellan bolted awake and grabbed for her gun when a hand gently shook her shoulder.

"It's me," Midnight hissed, and Kellan relaxed slightly. The elf was crouched at arm's length, and Kellan could just make out her features. Though Kellan had no idea what time it was, it clearly wasn't morning yet.

"Something's coming."

Kellan was about to ask what when she heard it: the distant sound of engines, high above, but getting closer. She threw aside the thermal blanket and scrambled to her feet. Shadows moving nearby told her the others were already awake.

"We need to—"

Before the words "take cover" could leave Kellan's mouth, a thunderbird LAV appeared over the treetops, turbofan engines roaring. A bright spotlight stabbed down into the clearing, ripping away the shadows and leaving the runners completely exposed and pinned in its glare. Kellan threw up a hand to shield her eyes from the blinding light.

As she wondered whether they should stand their ground or bolt for cover, the air shimmered and the translucent image of a woman dressed in a dark camo jumpsuit appeared. Her fiery red hair was cut short and dark wraparound glasses covered her eyes as she hovered a meter off the ground.

"Stay where you are," she commanded. Her voice carried easily over the noise of the LAV. Kellan realized it was because the voice was in her head, not her ears. "If you attempt to leave the area or if you take any hostile action toward the landing craft, we will respond with deadly force. Do you understand?"

"Who the frag are you?" Orion demanded and the woman's image turned to regard him coldly.

"Right now, I'm the woman who has about a million nuyen in ordnance aimed at you. Behave yourselves and I won't have to use it."

The elf warrior fell silent. Apparently satisfied that they were going to obey, the woman's image faded out.

The LAV banked in for a landing in the clearing. As it did so, Kellan could make out the red logo on its side: the stylized profile of an ancient Greek warrior wearing a plumed helmet.

"These guys are Ares!" she called out to Midnight, who nodded gravely.

Kellan's mind was racing. What was an Ares thunderbird doing out here in the middle of nowhere? Brickman worked for Knight Errant, which was a subsidiary of Ares Macrotechnology. Could he have sent the thunderbird and its crew as backup? If so, then why the hostile attitude? More importantly, how would Brickman even know where they were in order to send reinforcements?

Kellan covered her face with her arm to ward off the backwash from the thunderbird's thrusters, which sent up a spray of dirt and dead leaves before the pilot cut the engines and the LAV settled onto the ground. The side hatch opened and the woman whose image they had seen emerged in the flesh, accompanied by a half-dozen armed men in similar camo jumpsuits with the Ares logo on the shoulder and right breast. They wore sealed helmets with heads-up displays and carried Ares-made assault rifles at the ready.

"We are *royally* fragged," Draven muttered from somewhere behind Kellan as the troops approached.

"Captain Anna O'Connor, Ares Firewatch Team Epsilon," she announced, looking them over. "Who's in charge of this little group?" Natokah looked like he was going to reply, but Kellan stepped forward.

"I am."

O'Connor's eyebrows raised slightly above the edge of her shades as she looked Kellan over.

"Is that so?" she said. "Well then, would you like to explain who you are and what you're doing here?"

Kellan shrugged. "We're tourists," she began, but O'Connor cut her off with a sharp gesture.

"Cut the drek, kid," she said. "We know you're packing a lot more than camping gear, and we know some serious magic went down around here in the last twenty-four hours. Now we can play this one of two ways: either you can come clean and answer all of my questions, or I can drop all of you in a hole so deep and so dark that nobody will ever see you again. *Wakarimasuka?*"

"I think the Salish-Shidhe authorities might have something to say about that," Natokah stated, but O'Connor shook her head.

"No, they won't. I've got special authority to deal with certain . . . incidents in this area. As far as you're concerned, I'm God. Got it? Now, let's start again. Who are you, and what the frag are you *doing* here?"

Kellan swallowed with some effort and glanced at Midnight for support. O'Connor gestured curtly to her men, who advanced on the runners, weapons at the ready.

"Okay, okay!" Kellan said, "We're doing a job."

"What kind of job?"

"There . . . there was data on an old U.S. weapons cache," Kellan fumbled, nodding toward the excavated opening in the slope nearby. "We came looking for it."

The Ares commander looked around the makeshift camp. "I don't see any weapons."

"A guy named Zhade took them," Kellan replied.

"He just walked in and took these weapons? By himself?" she asked. Kellan couldn't tell if the Ares captain believed her or not; O'Connor's face was as impassive as stone.

"He was a spell-slinger," Kellan explained. "I think a shaman."

That seemed to get O'Connor's attention. Her brow furrowed. "A shaman?" she repeated. "What kind?"

Kellan shook her head but Natokah spoke up.

"Toxic," he said quietly. O'Connor snorted.

"Great," she muttered, "as if we didn't have enough to deal with." She turned to one of the men who stood nearby.

"Lieutenant, take a detachment and investigate this site," she told him and he snapped a salute in return, then went to do as ordered. "You," she said, turning back to the shadowrunners, "will stay right here until we assess the situation, which will give me a chance to make sure you're thoroughly checked out."

"For what?" Kellan asked, but she received no answer.

While some of the Ares personnel went to investigate the bunker, O'Connor had the shadowrunners stripped of their equipment, then examined each of them astrally. Kellan couldn't tell what the Ares officer was looking for, however. By the time her men returned, O'Connor had completed her astral scans and seemed satisfied with the results. Leaving some men to guard the runners, she moved off to confer with her second-in-command. While they were talking, an officer from the LAV brought O'Connor a message. She turned away from the lieutenant to speak briefly into her throat mic.

"What are they going to do with us?" Kellan asked Midnight, who was standing closest to her.

"I don't know," she replied. "If we're lucky, maybe Brickman can pull some strings—if he doesn't just deny having hired us."

"And if we're not lucky?"

Midnight didn't get a chance to answer that question as Captain O'Connor approached them again.

"Get them on board," she told the Ares guards, who gestured toward the LAV with their weapons.

"Where are you taking us?" Kellan asked.

"No talking—move!" one of the guards barked, his voice electronically filtered through speakers in his helmet. He gestured again with his rifle for emphasis, and Kellan had no choice but to move.

As soon as the shadowrunners were on board, the LAV fired up its engines. One of the Ares guards pulled the exterior hatch shut with a *thunk* that sounded through the cabin like a death knell in Kellan's ears. Now, there was no question: her first independent run had ended in complete failure. All she could do now was wait, and hope to survive the outcome.

20

The light in the dark room came from a fist-sized globe of greenish fire hovering about three meters above the floor. It cast a sickly glow over the accumulated trash, the rusting and decaying detritus of civilization that filled the room. The shaman Zhade bent over a workbench set against one wall, studying the maps laid out in front of him.

The shadows squeaked and chittered, and beady eyes reflected the greenish light as they watched the shaman at work.

"Soon, soon," Zhade murmured soothingly. "Everything is nearly ready." One gloved finger traced a path on the map, following a line he had drawn when the opportunity first presented itself.

"Soon," he repeated, "a part of the infestation in the body of the Mother will be no more. They will be seeing their last sunrise." His hand came to rest on the canisters liberated from the tribal lands, lovingly caressing the cold metal and flaking paint.

"I have everything I need now . . . everything."

To Kellan, it felt like the Ares LAV flew higher and faster than the *Leapin' Lizard* had on its way into Salish-Shidhe territory, though it was difficult to tell. The cabin had no windows, only blank flatscreen monitors. She assumed the Ares personnel had direct feeds from the HUD to their helmets, possibly even headware displays. She thought she caught a glimpse of light flickering behind the dark shades Captain O'Connor wore, too.

Although the cabin was larger than the *Lizard*'s, Kellan felt cramped and claustrophobic. Not only were there a good number more people crammed into it . . . Kellan had entered the Native American Nations a shadowrunner at the top of her game, and she was leaving them a prisoner. The guards had aggressively discouraged the shadowrunners from talking to each other, so Kellan just sat and stared at the wall, turning the whole thing over and over in her mind, trying to figure out where she'd gone wrong.

You know where you went wrong. You went wrong when you thought you were ready for this. She could barely admit it, even to herself. She *wasn't* ready to lead a team on her own. The disaster this run had become had proven it, and now her team was going to pay for her inexperience. *Well, I had enough experience to know that it is the leader's responsibility to solve problems: I'm still this team's leader, so it's up to me to find a solution to this situation.* She closed her eyes and considered. What did she have that she could use to bargain or negotiate?

There's Brickman, she thought. Brickman worked for a subsidiary of Ares, and Ares had captured them. Maybe dropping Brickman's name could get them out of this, if Captain O'Connor believed they were working for him. Of course, Brickman said he would disavow Kellan and her team if they were caught, so it was possible mentioning him would get them nothing. It would get even worse if Brickman was already implicated in something. In that case, confirming they were working for him would do more harm than good.

Brickman was the only leverage Kellan could think of, but she didn't want to waste the chance that he could help them by giving his name to O'Connor. If a connection with Brickman would get them in trouble, Kellan needed to know it. If Brickman could pull strings to help them out, she needed to get word to him. Of course, if he had set them up, then going to him directly would be dangerous. Assuming Kellan had the means to contact him at all . . .

It's useless, she thought angrily. Lothan was right. She should have listened to the troll mage when he came to her that night in her apartment, to warn her about Midnight and taking on this run. He—

That's it! It took every ounce of self control she possessed to keep her eyes closed, to slump against her seat like she'd gone to sleep. She figured it wouldn't take much to convince the guards that she was exhausted, given the way her body ached and what she knew she must look like on just a few hours sleep after all they'd gone through.

She took a deep breath and gently let it out, the tiny sound covered by the muffled thrumming of the engines. She concentrated.

The sensation was always like letting yourself fall. Kellan imagined it was like overcoming the natural aversion to jumping off a diving board or out of a plane, even if you knew there was water or a parachute to break your fall. She suddenly felt weightless, and there was a blur of light and motion, then she was soaring.

Kellan floated high in the air. She could see the rolling green of the land below, the night sky dappled with stars overhead. She looked around and saw the t-bird flying away, its running lights blinking. It took a moment to orient herself. Then she realized it was the first time she'd used astral projection from inside a moving vehicle—and one moving pretty fast, at that.

Of course—when I left my body, my astral form stayed at rest. The LAV passed right through me and kept going. Carrying her teammates, and her physical body, on toward their destination, wherever that was.

O'Connor had surely noticed Kellan's departure,

but apparently wasn't going to try to stop her. Of course, she had Kellan's body as the perfect hostage, knowing Kellan had to return eventually.

Kellan hoped she could find her body again. She'd learned the technique for returning to her body from Lothan, but she'd never before had to find her physical form—she'd only projected from a known and fixed location. Kellan couldn't afford to get lost, because she only had a limited time away from her body. Once the astral form left the physical form, the body began to die.

If I die, I'm not taking anyone with me.

Kellan soared higher. The earth dropped away below her, until she could see the glow of cities and towns, and even roads spread out like a map. She oriented on familiar landmarks and, with the speed of thought, arced toward the Seattle Metroplex, covering hundreds of kilometers in a matter of a few minutes.

Once she reached the metroplex, it was easy to navigate her way to a particular house on Capitol Hill. She slowed and approached the shimmering wards covering the walls of the building, placing one ghostly hand against them and sending out a call, like a psychic knock on the door. The seconds seemed to drag past, then the surface of the ward rippled and parted, forming a gateway that allowed her to enter.

She found Lothan in his study, as she'd expected. She couldn't tell if she'd awakened him from a sound sleep or if he was maintaining his typical nocturnal habits; he seemed completely unperturbed by her interruption, and unsurprised to see her.

"Yes, Kellan, what is it?"

Kellan hovered in the middle of the room for a moment. "Lothan, I—I need your help. I don't have much time."

Her mentor's demeanor changed immediately. He turned from whatever it was he was reading on his desk to face Kellan directly.

"Tell me, then," he said, "quickly."

So she did. She told Lothan about getting backing for the run from Brickman, arranging to get into Salish-Shidhe territory, finding the chemical weapons, their encounter with the shaman Zhade, and the arrival of the Ares team. She braced herself for a lecture, a few acerbic words of recrimination—even for Lothan to dismiss her tale of woe and send her on her way, telling her she'd made her bed and now had to lie in it.

The troll mage did none of those things. Instead, he immediately got to his feet, picked up his staff from its customary resting place and lifted his heavy overcoat from its hook.

"Return to your body as quickly as you can, and don't leave it again until you hear from me. Let me look into a few things. Just sit tight and don't try anything foolish." She turned to leave and Lothan called after her.

"And Kellan?"

"Yeah?"

"Don't worry. Everything will be all right."

She paused for a moment, taking in the sober look of confidence on the old troll's lined face, then she nodded.

"Thanks, Lothan."

Slipping out through the wards on the house, Kellan concentrated on feeling the familiar pulse of her heart, the heaviness of her limbs. She focused and felt the faint, almost infinitesimal tug of her physical form, the unbreakable connection between body and spirit, and began to home in on it.

It was slower going than Kellan expected. She cast around often, trying to make sure she was going the right way, careful to not overshoot in any direction. The lights of the metroplex faded in the distance, giving way to the wilderness of the tribal lands. Finally, she saw the running lights of the LAV in the distance. The closer she got, the stronger she felt the connection to her body, like it was drawing her in. In a rush, she flew into the thunderbird, the world spun, and she opened her eyes.

"Welcome back," Captain O'Connor said in an acid tone, glaring at Kellan from across the cabin. "I was wondering if you were going to bother to return, or if you'd checked out for good."

"I said she would be back," Orion defended her, but Kellan could hear the relief in his voice.

"So, did you have a nice trip?" The Ares mage held Kellan's gaze for long minutes before she shrugged. "Doesn't matter, really, whether you tipped someone off or were trying to call in reinforcements. Frankly, I don't give a flying frag about whatever game you're playing. Once I deliver you to Seattle, you're not my problem anymore."

"Seattle?" Kellan asked.

"Naturally. Where did you think we were going? I told you, I've got a job to finish back in Hell's Canyon, so I'm making you somebody else's problem."

21

It only took a few hours for the Ares t-bird to arrive in the Seattle Metroplex. Landing clearance was arranged—not at Sea-Tac Airport, but at a private airfield owned and operated by Ares for corporate commuter flights.

The shadowrunners were ushered out of the thunderbird into an almost featureless room, the door closed and locked behind them.

"What do you think they're—?" Orion began, but Midnight hushed him with a shake of her head and a finger held to her lips. She waved that finger toward the ceiling vaguely, indicating there might be listening devices in the room. It was likely they were being observed, and that someone was just waiting for them to say something interesting. The shadowrunners all got the message: better to remain silent than to give away what little they might be able to bargain with later.

So they sat and waited in silence. Kellan considered using astral projection again but decided not to risk it. O'Connor might not have been interested in stopping her, but the magical security of the Ares facility might feel differently. Plus, there was no one besides Lothan to contact. So they waited.

When the door of the room opened again, Simon Brickman stood there, a thunderous look distorting his usually bland expression. Rather than the fashionable business attire Kellan had seen him in previously, he was dressed in dark jeans and a close-fitting tee-shirt under a synthleather jacket equipped with armored padding and inserts. Dark shades covered his eyes, and he wore black wrist-length gloves.

"Come with me," he ordered, and turned away from the open door.

"What about our gear?" Orion asked, and Brickman spun back.

"Do not make me regret getting you out of here," he said through clenched teeth. He turned and walked away. Brickman led them into one of the airfield administrative buildings and straight to a conference room. The runners were surprised to find Lothan waiting there. The troll mage stood on the far side of the table, leaning on his staff, because none of the chairs were large enough for him.

Brickman closed the door behind them and made sure the blinds fully covered the windows. Then he took a small triangular device from the inside pocket of his jacket, checked its readout, and set it against the door just over the knob, where it clung with a click.

"Sit," he said, as if he were speaking to a bad dog, and pointed at the conference table. The shadowrunners warily sat in the chairs closest to Brickman.

"This has been quite possibly the worst frag-up to which I've ever been connected," Brickman began.

"It wasn't our—" Kellan began.

"I don't want to hear it!" the Ares company man barked. "I don't care. All I care about is making sure my name isn't connected with any more of this drek." He glanced at Lothan, who simply watched and listened. "Fraggit," Brickman went on. "Hell's Canyon?" he asked. "Of all the places you could have gone . . ."

"What's the big deal about Hell's Canyon?" Kellan asked.

"It's classified," Brickman said. "So classified that even *I* don't know what it's about. All I know is that the area is so important that the Salish-Shidhe government has had a special arrangement with Ares for the past eight years regarding it. The area is constantly patrolled by elite Firewatch teams, who are authorized to bust anyone who shows up there."

"There's no way we could have known that."

Brickman snorted. "The sad part is, nobody would have known you were there if you'd done the job properly."

"It wasn't our fault!" Kellan said, smacking the table. "Zhade—"

"Ah, yes, Zhade," Brickman said. "Who got hold of your supposedly 'secret' data, who showed up right behind you at the fraggin' site, and who took the goods right out from under you. Apparently I should have hired him!"

Kellan yanked Brickman's credstick out of her jacket pocket and slammed it down on the table.

"Yeah? Well you can take your fraggin' cred and—"

"Enough," Lothan said. "Recriminations are pointless. What happened, happened. We need to move on."

Brickman straightened up from where he'd been leaning over the table and glared at Lothan.

"It's not quite that simple," he said. "There's still the small matter of Zhade, and what he took."

"What of it?" Midnight interjected.

"Under most circumstances, I wouldn't give a frag," Brickman replied. "But in this case, we all know that Zhade will use those chemicals, most likely right here in the metroplex. It's not going to be hard to track the source of the poison back to this team, and I don't trust you to be discreet; therefore, it will be traced to me. That, I can't afford, and won't tolerate. So it's this simple: you are going to stop Zhade and recover the chemicals."

"Fine," Midnight replied, relaxing in her chair. "What's it worth to you?"

Brickman's ghost of a smile sent a chill down Kellan's spine. "Oh, no," he said softly. "It doesn't work that way this time. As long as it's possible for any of this to be traced to me, it's in all our best interests to see to it that Zhade is deprived of any opportunity to use his swag. Because you will go down before I will. And you will go down in flames."

There was a long moment of utter silence.

"How do we find him?" Kellan asked. Brickman turned his attention back to her.

"That's where you come in."

"This isn't going to work," Kellan said for the twentieth time.

"Not with that attitude it won't," Lothan agreed. "If you don't want me to do this with you, I can go. . . ."

"Sorry," Kellan muttered. "I'm just not feeling too confident right now."

"Kellan, you made a mistake—"

"There's a newsflash."

Lothan silenced Kellan with a hard look. "You made a mistake," he repeated. "But now you have a chance to do something to correct it—a rare opportunity."

Kellan nodded. "Yeah. I do appreciate your help with this, Lothan."

"Are you ready to get to work?"

Since they all agreed that Zhade would use the chemicals rather than sell them, they planned to use a small sample of the stolen chemicals to find the remaining canisters, and thus the toxic shaman. The

Firewatch team had given Brickman a sample of the poisonous substance from the bunker. It was, as Squeak had suspected, an old chemical weapon that the United States had been unwilling to deploy during the Ghost Dance War. When your enemy could control the wind and weather, such weapons could only prove ineffective, and dangerous to everyone involved.

The magical principle of contagion postulated that there was a deep, unbreakable connection between the parts of an object and the whole. Magicians could use samples of blood, hair, or nail parings—a small part of the whole person—to cast spells against human and metahuman targets from half a world away. The same principle applied to inanimate objects: an element separated from the whole could be used to find the other part.

Kellan understood the theory and had studied the ritual used to perform this magical task, but she had never actually tried to find something this way. She would need Lothan's help, which was precisely why Brickman had agreed to the other mage's presence.

"This won't be easy," Lothan warned her. "Zhade may be mad, but everything I've heard indicates that he's a very capable magician. Odds are, he'll have defenses erected, and he may even be prepared for magical attempts to locate him."

"Well, Zhade thinks we're dead," Kellan replied. "Hopefully that'll give us an edge."

In the interest of making best use of every available

moment, Brickman agreed to let them perform the ritual at Lothan's house, since he stocked everything they needed in his workshop. Lothan had removed the summoning circle he had used in his demonstration for Kellan's lesson only a few days before, so they were able to prepare the ritual space relatively quickly. Kellan consulted Lothan's grimoires for the necessary symbols to inscribe around and between the ritual circles. Lothan insisted on Kellan getting some rest before they started, saying she would be no use to the process if she failed in the middle of the ritual from exhaustion. Kellan did her best to meditate quietly for a little while as Lothan gathered the necessary incense, herbs, candles and other ingredients of the ritual.

When everything was ready, they began. Kellan lit the candles and ignited some charcoal for the small incense burner, then gently poured some ground incense onto the coals. It sent up a thin stream of smoke smelling of sandalwood, myrrh and frankincense. Lothan took the censer and ritually swept out the circle to banish all unwanted and negative energies. Kellan set the incense on a stand in the middle of the circle next to a small iron cauldron filled with clear spring water.

Standing together in the middle of the ritual space, face-to-face, the two mages created a circle with their arms around the cauldron. Together they raised the power of the circle, consecrating it as their place of working, creating a barrier between them and the mundane world as well as a protective ward around them on the astral plane. They invited the powers of the four directions and the four elements to join them in the circle, to support their work. With Lothan guiding and supporting her, Kellan felt a small part of her confidence returning as she spoke the familiar words that formed the beginning of every ritual.

Kellan picked up the small, sealed sample vial Brickman had given her. She held it out in the palm of her hand and Lothan held his hand over it, so that their flesh surrounded the chemical. They focused their thoughts on the vial, and Kellan spoke the words of their intent.

"Through this poison," she said, "we reach out to that which was taken, but always connected, part of the whole." Kellan felt the power building and took hold of it, directing it into the sample they held, using it to strengthen the connection between it and the remaining canisters of chemicals. "By our will is the connection made manifest, by our power is it made clear. Show us the way, show us the path we seek. So be it!"

The energy spun out like threads of faerie light, infinitely fine, as if made from the swirling smoke rising from the incense. Kellan used one hand to gently play them out, casting them into astral space. She concentrated on the threads, making them an extension of her will. They stretched out like feelers, searching blindly. It was slow, delicate work that required Kellan's complete concentration to maintain and strengthen each connection.

Then she felt it. A faint tug shivering through one thread. Contact.

"There it is," she heard Lothan say softly.

Kellan opened her eyes as Lothan raised his hand. She took the vial of chemicals and gently dropped it into the water in the cauldron. The surface of the water turned black almost instantly. Kellan gazed at the ripples on the dark surface of the water. Reflected candlelight gleamed, and smoke drifted across it like fog. As the ripples shimmered, Kellan could see an image forming, becoming more distinct as each moment passed.

"I can't see exactly where it is," she told Lothan. The troll came to stand behind Kellan, gently placing his hands on her shoulders.

"Allow the vision to widen," he said softly, "and draw back."

Kellan did as he said, rolling back the perspective on her vision like a camera pulling back from its subject, her point of view widening out. She saw a dingy, dimly lit building—a warehouse. Pulling back farther, she saw its dilapidated exterior and great mounds, mountains, of trash and refuse stretching into the distance.

"It's a dump," she said, "a huge landfill."

"The Rat's Nest," Lothan said.

"I can see the building," Kellan said, "but I can't see inside; there's not enough light."

"Don't force it. Better to just come back. Let the image go."

Kellan released her vision, and it was like waking from a dream. Lothan took a ritual dagger and passed it over the cauldron, severing the connection they had created, so it couldn't be traced back to them. Then they carefully grounded the remaining energy.

The rest of the team was waiting in Lothan's study. They looked up expectantly as the two mages walked in.

"The Rat's Nest," Kellan announced. "I can lead us to Zhade's hideout."

"Makes sense," Orion said. "Where else are you going to find a trash-rat like Zhade?"

"Good," Brickman replied. "Now we deal with Zhade and recover the goods."

"We?" Kellan asked.

"Of course," he said. "You can't seriously believe I'd let this team out of my sight again. I want to make sure it gets done *right* this time."

Kellan swallowed the response she wanted to make and nodded.

"Fine," she said. "Let's do it."

22

The door splintered under Draven's and Orion's combined weight, crashing onto the dusty floor.

"Go!" Brickman ordered, and the shadowrunners covered each other as they entered the warehouse Kellan had pinpointed. The interior was dim, the only light coming from the doorway.

Orion and Draven split off left, Midnight and Natokah went right. Kellan and Brickman headed straight. They moved from door to door, weaving around piles of trash, coming in high and low to cover each room. In a few minutes, they all met in the large central room.

"Anything?" Kellan asked, and the others shook their heads.

"Nothing here but trash," Orion said.

"Look," Midnight pointed.

A wide workbench took up half of one wall. Underneath it, resting on top of a stack of rolled cloth was a canister. Kellan examined it carefully.

"This is definitely one of the canisters from the bunker," she said. "But where're the rest of them, and Zhade?"

"Quiet," Orion said, cocking his head. "What's that noise?"

Kellan heard it, a skittering and high-pitched squeaking.

"Over there?" She thought she saw something move in the shadows, then suddenly they came.

A horde of rats, dozens of them, came pouring out of the darkness. They were each nearly a meter long. Their pale bodies were almost hairless, covered in scabs and sores, and their beady eyes seemed to burn with a reddish light. They hissed and squealed and bared their fangs as they swarmed the shadowrunners.

"Devil rats!" Draven shouted. He swung the new axe Brickman had supplied when he liberated the rest of their weapons from Ares, neatly cutting one of the charging rats in half. The dwarf's weapon sang in a deadly arc to fend off the attacking creatures.

The shadowrunners stood back-to-back near the workbench. Midnight and Brickman both fired on the rats, the elf taking precise, deadly shots, the company man firing his submachine gun in short bursts that pulped the animals.

Orion and Draven wielded sword and axe like exterminators, hacking and slashing with great efficiency.

Natokah stepped close to Kellan, leaned in and pitched his voice to be heard over the racket. "Manaball!"

Kellan nodded, then they turned and faced opposite corners of the room. The shaman chanted, his voice rising to a penetrating cry that echoed in the room. Kellan spoke the words she had learned to focus the power for her spell, shouting the final phrase. Light flickered in the shadows in a soundless explosion, and half the remaining devil rats fell unmoving to the floor.

With the bulk of the devil rats dead from Kellan's and Natokah's spell, the other shadowrunners quickly finished off the rest. Orion yanked his sword from the last of the monstrous rats, wiping the blade off with a rag he tossed on the floor as Draven leaned on his axe and looked over the carnage.

"Devil rats," he grunted, "disgusting fraggers. Figures Zhade would keep 'em like pets."

Kellan had already turned back to the workbench, which had scattered printouts spread across it.

"Look at this," she said, and the others gathered closer as Kellan picked up a sheet of flimsy paper.

"Maps," Brickman said.

"They show the stops along the monorail system," Kellan continued. "And here's a schedule of when the trains run."

"Oh, frag," Draven muttered.

"What?" Orion asked.

"It looks like Zhade is planning to spread this stuff using the trains," Midnight explained.

"He could take out a good part of the downtown area in a pretty short amount of time," Draven added.

Kellan had already reached that conclusion, and was studying the maps and diagrams, desperate to find a pattern to the markings—something to indicate where Zhade planned to make his move.

"Here," she said abruptly, pointing to a spot on the map. "This station has the heaviest circle around it. It must be where Zhade is going."

"That's a pretty big hunch, Kellan." Midnight stared thoughtfully at the map. "But I agree with you. If I were going to try to kill a lot of people efficiently, that would be a good place to start."

Kellan turned to Brickman. "You have to tell Lone Star so they can stop him."

"Tell them what?" he replied, incredulous. "That there's a madman on the loose with a chemical weapon you rightfully stole before he took it from you? For starters, they wouldn't believe me. And even if they did decide to take me seriously, they wouldn't move fast enough to stop Zhade in time. Finally, I don't want Lone Star connecting me with this, so I'm sure as hell not going to give them the connection!"

"You wanted to recover the goods. Well, we can't do that. So now we've got to stop him doing whatever it is he's planning to do," Kellan nearly shouted, flourishing the map in her fist. "You may not be willing to sacrifice your reputation to save lives, but I'll fraggin' sacrifice it for you if that's what it takes to get you to do the right thing! And I don't care if I go down first!"

Brickman gave Kellan that smile again, the one that sent chills down her spine back in the conference room at the airport. But this time she was angry, and she refused to be intimidated.

"It's fortunate for you, Ms. Colt, that your threats coincide with my own plans." He turned away and pulled out his cell phone.

Less than fifteen minutes later, they were in an unmarked helicopter on their way to downtown Seattle. Kellan looked out the window at the lights of the metroplex, hoping they would be in time, hoping that she had guessed right. They were heading the direction in which the clues had pointed them; had they read the clues correctly? Was Zhade even making his move tonight?

As they approached the station, they could see that something was happening. Pedestrians were running away from the monorail station, and no one was boarding or leaving the train. The pilot and Brickman talked briefly, and the helicopter headed toward a building near the station platform. Brickman turned to the runners. "It will add a minute to our time, but we're going to set down on that building"—he pointed—"and go down the exterior fire escape. We can't jump directly onto the platform from the 'copter with that thing in our way." A huge, hulking creature that looked like a living mass of garbage and toxic waste occupied the center of the boarding platform, surrounded by hideously burned bodies.

Kellan didn't bother to object, because there didn't seem to be any better option. The runners shot out of the helicopter before it actually settled on the roof and ran for the fire escape, making it to street level in record time. Kellan took the two flights of stairs up to the platform two steps at a time, with Orion right on her heels.

The carnage was horrifying. The bodies of would-be passengers littered the platform, and many more of Zhade's victims lay thrown about in the monorail cars. As Kellan struggled to comprehend the sheer number of dead, she saw Zhade. At the same moment, the shaman spotted her, and the spirit lunged forward.

"Zhade!" Kellan bellowed, charging toward the open doors of the train. Orion leapt between her and the toxic spirit, slashing at it with his sword, holding it at bay.

Kellan swung in through the doors, pulling out her pistol. Zhade pointed at her and sneered, "You're supposed to be dead." A stream of acid sprayed from his outstretched hand. Kellan reflexively deflected a portion of the spell's energy, but not before the acid burned holes in her armored jacket and pitted and melted her pistol. Kellan tossed it aside. She kept moving toward Zhade and raised her hand. When he instinctively made a warding gesture, Kellan dropped low and lashed out with a leg sweep she'd learned from Orion. The blow knocked the shaman off his feet and back into the seats.

She heard the other shadowrunners pound up onto the platform, and Natokah began singing a banishment against the toxic spirit. Kellan kept her advantage, leaping onto Zhade and grabbing what she could of the front of his clothes.

"The poison!" she demanded, and Zhade laughed.

"You're too late." A musical tone sounded over the train's speakers.

"Kellan, the doors!" Orion shouted. As the car doors began to close, he dove through them, tucking into a roll as he hit the floor of the car. Midnight made an equally elegant dive through the closing train doors as the monorail lurched and began to move.

Kellan only turned her attention away from Zhade for a second, but the toxic shaman slammed the heel of his hand into her chin, breaking her hold and sending her reeling.

Orion raised his sword and charged Zhade with a blood-curdling cry. The shaman gestured and Orion slammed full tilt into a mystic barrier that sprang up between them, separating the two halves of the monorail car. He took a step back, then hacked at the barrier with his sword. The blade sliced through slowly but surely, like cutting wet clay.

It was Kellan's turn to take advantage of a momentary distraction. Zhade turned his attention back toward Kellan just as she jabbed him with her stun baton. There was a sizzling *crack* and Zhade cried out in pain and fury, but he stayed on his feet. He swatted the weapon out of Kellan's hand, sending it clattering to the floor. The glowing magical wall suddenly collapsed.

Kellan yelled, "Stop the train!" and Midnight ran for the control booth.

"It's over, Zhade!" Kellan said. "Give it up and you might just walk away from this."

"Never!" he screamed. "Not until I silence the Earth's pain! Not until I kill the parasites infesting her—parasites like you!" He raised his arms above his head, and she could see the glow of gathering power.

"Orion, look out!" Kellan extended her magical defenses, trying to block Zhade's spell as the shaman hurled a small sphere of energy toward them. The blast shook the monorail and blew out part of the wall of the car. The wind roared around the car's interior as they continued to pick up speed, skimming over the charged track below.

Kellan managed to grab on to one of the upright supports, but Orion wasn't so lucky. Though she was able to shield both of them from the force of the blast, Orion slid toward the hole in the wall as the train took a curve. He drove his sword through one of the seats and held tightly to the hilt to avoid being flung out of the car.

"Orion!" Kellan swung out from the support pole, stretching out her hand, allowing Orion to grab hold and stabilize himself. She was aware of Zhade beginning another spell as she helped pull Orion to his feet.

"Die!" the shaman shouted, and as the train took a curve in the opposite direction Orion stumbled across the car, pushing Kellan back, and was hit by the stream of acid intended for her. There was a sizzling sound as Orion dropped to his knees, screaming in pain. His sword fell from suddenly nerveless fingers to slide under the seats as he collapsed onto the floor.

Zhade circled into the middle of the car as Kellan pushed herself up out of the seat she'd fallen into. She looked down at Orion's body, smoke rising from the bubbling acid wound across his back.

"Bastard!" she screamed. Kellan poured her fury into a roaring streamer of flames. Zhade held out one hand, deflecting the fire like it was spray of water from a hose. With his other hand, he conjured a shard of energy that he hurled at Kellan like a dagger. She batted it away as if it were an annoying insect.

"You're more powerful than I expected," Zhade said. "But you're no match for me. The corruption of the world is my weapon, and you've given me the key to increase my power beyond anything you can imagine!"

The toxic shaman pressed the attack, greenish lightning crackling from his hands. Kellan deflected it, but she knew Zhade was right. He was more powerful than she, and Kellan knew she couldn't stand up to his assault much longer.

Maybe I can't beat this fragger, but he is not *going to win.* She reinforced her defenses, then began gathering the power she would need for a blast that would take out the monorail car and everything in it. She recalled Brickman's words to her.

"You're going down before I do," she said to Zhade, "and you're going down in flames."

She realized that she didn't need to shout to be heard: the wind was dying down, because the monorail was slowing. Zhade noticed it, too.

"No!" the shaman howled, and Kellan grinned in triumph.

"That means Midnight got control of the train."

A shot echoed in the car.

"Got it under control," Midnight said from the doorway, her pistol still leveled at Zhade.

The shaman stumbled back a step as blood began to leak between the pieces of his makeshift armor.

"Down . . ." he muttered, "down in flames." He raised his hands, greenish flames flickering into being around them, and Midnight fired twice more. Fire streaked toward Kellan, but she deflected it with ease. The shaman's fearsome power was gone. The impact of the two shots in quick succession sent Zhade stumbling toward the blasted wall of the car. He overstepped and reached for some kind of handhold, but his hands found only empty air where the side of the monorail car had been. He windmilled his arms for a second, balanced there, then the monorail took a curve and the shaman plunged toward the street below. His scream was lost in the wind and the squeal of the wheels on the track.

Epilogue

"**W**e got clear of the train before Lone Star showed up," Kellan said, "so there weren't any witnesses to what happened, and it's a pretty sure thing that Zhade's not going to be talking to anyone."

Simon Brickman relaxed in his desk chair with a look of smug satisfaction. Kellan Colt and Midnight occupied the chairs in front of him, and Lothan the Wise stood behind them.

"Good," Brickman said. "This debacle hasn't turned out to be a total loss, after all. I've been able to spin things so that rumors 'leaked' to the press suggest Knight Errant thwarted plans by terrorists to unleash a deadly chemical weapon on the metroplex, and that we recovered the remaining weapons to turn them over to the UCAS government. It's enough to keep Lone Star scrambling to explain why they didn't find out about this threat until it was too late for them to do anything about it."

"Glad we could help." Brickman chuckled at the sarcasm in Kellan's voice.

"I wouldn't complain if I were you," he said. "After all, I allowed you to keep the cred I provided to cover your expenses, and Natokah and Lothan were able to see to it that there were no significant medical bills. Speaking of which, how is Orion?"

"He'll be fully recovered with a few more days' rest," Lothan said.

"He's a lucky young man."

"Then we're square?" Kellan asked, and Brickman nodded.

"I'd say our business is concluded."

"Good." Kellan stood.

"Go ahead," Midnight said to her. "I'll be right there."

Kellan looked at Brickman for a moment, then nodded and left the room. Lothan gave Brickman and Midnight each a measured stare before turning to follow Kellan out the door. When the door closed behind Lothan, Brickman regarded Midnight with a faint smile.

"I want to know that you aren't going to give her any trouble over this," Midnight said, and Brickman's smile widened into a smirk.

"Why, Midnight, do I sense an attachment to this kid?" he asked. "You never struck me as the mentoring type." She shrugged.

"You said it yourself. Kellan has considerable potential—she just needs the training and experience to go with it."

"And you're the one to give it to her?"

"Who better? After all, I have been playing this game for a long time, Simon."

"Yes," Brickman said. "Sometimes, I think longer than you let on. But it still doesn't explain why you'd burden yourself by taking on an apprentice, Midnight. Thinking of retiring?"

The elf woman smiled. "You know shadowrunners don't retire, Brickman." Her expression turned serious again. "Just tell me things are really square."

"They're square," Brickman replied. "I wouldn't hire that kid to escort my mother across the street, let alone trust her with my shadow business. I give her one, maybe two more runs before she turns up dead in the sprawl."

Satisfied, Midnight turned to leave.

"If you ask me, you're wasting your time, Midnight."

She turned to regard the Ares company man coldly. "You do business your way, I'll do it mine."

When the door closed behind Midnight, Simon Brickman leaned back in his chair. He needed to figure out how to take the momentary advantage over Lone Star and parlay it into something he could use, but he took a few minutes to consider Midnight's interest in Kellan Colt.

She was right: shadowrunners didn't retire. Unless they managed to hit the big score, they worked the shadows until time and age caught up with them and they made a fatal mistake. Certainly, Midnight had the ambition to hit the big score.

Just how did Kellan Colt figure in?

ABOUT THE AUTHOR

Steve Kenson stepped into the shadows in 1997 with the *Awakenings* sourcebook. Since then he has written or contibuted to more than two dozen Shadowrun® RPG books. His first Shadowrun novel, *Technobabel*, was published in 1998. He has written four other Shadowrun novels (*Crossroads, Ragnarock, The Burning Time*, and *Born to Run*), in addition to MechWarrior® and Crimson Skies™ novels. Stephen lives in Merrimack, New Hampshire, with his partner, Christopher Penczak.